OUT THERE

VOLUME 2

B. A. PAUL

CONTENTS

FOREWORD

I love science fiction. Give me bioengineered dinosaurs running amok. Beam me up to a spherical space station in the great beyond. Transport me to dystopian societies so I can see how bad things can really get.

Pack my bags and let me time travel away from my current reality—even if I end up a little worse for the wear, at least I'll have had a new experience and the bragging rights of learning proper portal protocols.

Even my Little Miss Muse prefers tiptoeing and pirouetting with her purple tutu through alternate realities. Her impish wings flitter and flick with sheer adrenaline when I tell her it's time to fire up the idea factory for a science fiction short. Lavender glitter erupts from her very essence, the three felines go running for cover, and she even breaks out her bottle rockets.

I hope you enjoy reading these tales as much as I—um, I mean *Little Miss Muse* and I—enjoyed writing them.

Apologies in advance for any purple glitter left in the pages...

(Discover all the Little Miss Muse antics on the blog at bapaul.com—and the three cats, too.)

Happy Reading!

B. A. Paul

p.s. This volume is dedicated to Little Miss Muse who reminded me (not so gently) that she's due all the credit for the Writers of the Future Honorable Mention awarded to "The Shades."

Thank you, Little Miss. What would I do without you?

THE SHADES

Awarded Honorable Mention by Writers of the Future, The Shades explores how far one little boy will go to calm the fear of the person he loves the most...

Fletcher Mayfield sat the galvanized water bucket next to the generator, slowly. Since the first time he'd felt baby Faith kick inside his mother's stomach, he'd slowed all his movements. He rubbed his hands over his backside. His pants were tighter in the rear than they had been since that first kick. His parents thought him to be ill. Fletcher smiled.

He wasn't ill; he was simply puttin' on.

Puttin' on and nearly old enough to do something about it.

He bent to check the generator's brick count. Four, maybe five left, according to the blinking orange triangle on the gauge. It seemed foolish to use precious electricity to power the fuel gauges. Dad ranted about it constantly. Someone surely could figure out a mechanical means of keeping track of the juice in the genny. But no one had.

Rich and poor, Towners and Shaders wasted countless combined bricks every day to tell them how many bricks they had left. Spent energy that could pour candles or weave longer lasting wicks. Or power the machines to sew warm socks.

Two Canada geese, late for the flying V formation Fletcher had spotted earlier in the day, flapped and squawked over the subdivision, aiming for the nearly bare treetop line in the distance. Maybe when Faith was old enough, the Mayfields could follow those geese to warmer weather and longer days.

And socks wouldn't be so top-of-mind.

Winter was coming. Thick socks would be nice. The days would be shorter, so longer-lasting wicks would be nice too. Fletcher—nine years old, ten in a week—despised the dark. And Faith, ripe old age of nine days, was shaping up to follow in big brother's footsteps.

His family, his entire cul-de-sac had pooled their voter cards to request that SoLar produce such practical items. Socks. Candles. Buckets, even, come to think of it. The factory's labor was supplied by the people of the Shades, after all, and the people of the Shades should have some say in what goods came out of the factory.

It didn't much matter. For the fall quarter run, the Towners' votes won out, as they usually did, and the good workers of SoLar would churn out yet another run of vanity items. Toothbrushes, combs, and razors.

None of which help families with the freezing cold. Or the heavy black of night.

Fletcher checked the cords and connections on the generator like his dad had shown him to do. He wanted to be inside the safety of the house before the sun dipped past the rooftops and drowned out rays over the horizon. No cloud cover today, though. Perhaps the wind would stay to the north and leave their skies clear. Scant stars to guide them through their home.

The remaining four bricks—called such because the stacked red rectangles on the government-issued generators looked like building blocks, each linking to the next—would last the family another day or so if they were very careful. Until Dad brought home his paycheck in the form of a charging block. With a partial allotment of bricks. For one week's work making toothbrushes and combs and razors for the good folks of the town.

If Faith behaved herself tonight the bricks may last. If she freaked out with the dipping of the sun, like she had the last couple of nights, maybe not.

The water pail in hand and the generator checked, he went through to the kitchen. Slowly. Conserving his calories as best he could. He could see his mother nursing Faith, a tiny balled fist escaping the green swaddle blanket. Mom couldn't take her eyes off her daughter during these times, and she didn't see Fletcher staring. Fletcher wished he could sit next to them on the sofa and listen to Faith's baby noises and let her tiny pink fingers curl around his dirty ones.

But he had chores and his duty to conserve the bricks. He'd get his turn with Faith after dinner when the sun disappeared. He felt a connection to his sister during the night hours—even before she was born. He felt the fear she had of the dark—the same terror tingles that pricked the back of his neck likely pricked her tiny body too. They shared this. Fletcher felt together they could help get through the dark hours of the Shades.

And, someday, he'd teach her not to be envious of the Towners with their giant generators and extra bricks just pouring out of their ears. Keeping the lights on all night in the city while the suburbs in all directions—packed with hungry, cold, and brick-conserving families such as his—waited in the town's shade until the earth spun once more and bathed the long-ago, well-off neighborhoods in precious light.

What a luxury the Towners had. The Shaders, well. "Conservation is the king," Dad had said. "One day, one day. They'll break the grid again with their greediness and the Shaders will reign with their practicality and conservation skills. You wait and see."

Fletcher dumped the water into the giant crock on the wood stove and retrieved another pail full for the sink. A third trip gave the family an extra bucketful—a bucket dangerously close to cracking—for the night hours.

He'd write down water pail on his list of ideas for the winter quarter vote. Socks would remain on as well. Fletcher was barefoot and near blistered in his one-size-too-big boots.

A small price to pay to conserve bricks.

Just last week Mom had struggled to maneuver her gravid belly around the cast iron cook stove and the single dining chair. He'd never seen anything like that stomach in the Shades. Pregnancies were rare, and when the phenomenon did occur, most women thought themselves puttin' on instead of expecting, sending them skipping off to CellLite for a turn in the chair and a full allotment or two of bricks—worth a man's entire month of work, it was.

Just one trip to CellLite.

And one had to be double digits to sit in the chair.

Double digits and puttin' on.

Thank the heavens Mom knew the difference between baby belly and pooch, though. Fletcher became a big brother for the first time ever and the only big brother his age that he knew of in the whole of their subdivision. And he'd planned on being the best big brother a baby could have.

Mom had taken to dragging a dining chair over the cracked tile floor of the kitchen to have a rest in between the food prep and the dish washing. She still did this, dragging the chair, even after Faith came. She was always fussing with the food prep and washing up. Doing her best to preserve bricks. Push their allotments a little further into the week.

The whole family was cautious. Anything with a cord that wasn't necessary for survival had been removed from their home altogether before Fletcher was even born. Other items deemed useful were left unplugged. Electronics like phones and things with screens that once held sounds and motion and music were gone. If the Mayfields or their neighbors wanted music, they'd use their own voices and bang on a bucket for rhythm.

If it was entertainment they craved, they'd make their own, reading from books or making up stories, or, on very rare occasions, trek into the town and spend a few bricks for someone else to tickle their fancy. Most of the Shaders Fletcher knew, however, kept to the Shades save for the trek to SoLar for their work shifts.

And it had been ages since anyone he knew trekked to CellLite. Everyone Fletcher knew was fit and trim—or downright gaunt—from hard work, prior CellLite visits, or constant brick-level worry.

Everyone except Fletcher.

His pants were tight.

Mom did have the baby fat. But she said she'd keep that to help feed Faith. Her body would burn it quickly enough nursing, and with Fletcher and Dad's help, they'd make do with the bricks Dad earned at SoLar. Avoid a trip to the chair for Mom.

Fletcher was relieved at this decision. Babies were precious, and Faith needed a strong start. Much more than the Mayfields' home needed the bricks from a CellLite harvest.

And he'd heard it was painful, those trips in the chair. Not right away, but later. During the recovery when one should be enjoying the fruits of extra bricks, the suction incisions in the hips and stomach would sometimes ooze and swell, costing more in bricks for a medical appointment than what was gained by the harvest of the cellulite to begin with.

But Fletcher was young and would rebound quickly. And most of his harvest, he guessed would come from his rear, not his belly. And who had time to sit down with a new baby to look after?

Broom in hand, Fletcher tidied up the broken bits and dust of the ceramic tile. He did this slowly, so as not to spend calories he couldn't afford. Always conserving.

The home's age and the dragging of the chair chipped the floor a bit more each day. He scooted the broom near the fridge and caught a few more loose pieces with the bristles. The refrigerator with levers in the door for water and ice remained unplugged. Fletcher could only imagine what it would be like to fill a glass of water from that door. And ice? No ice meant constant food prep. Fix only enough to stifle the hunger pangs and have no waste. None.

The glass shelves inside, Dad said, would light up if you plugged it in. And all the food on one side would stay just so cold, like a cool, spring morning. And the other side would freeze like the dead of winter. In all of Fletcher's days, the refrigerator had never been plugged in and only served as an extra cabinet for sugar and flour and random pots and pans.

Fletcher put Mom's chair back at the dining table before Dad came home, frail and hungry, his coveralls glistening with shards of metal shavings and solar panel treatments and remnants of tooth-brush bristles.

Mom had left a potato casserole to warm on the back of the wood-stove, and Fletcher placed it on the table. Even though it would mean extra shifts, Dad had wished that Mom switch over to the stainless-steel cooktop during the last part of her pregnancy. He'd get a neighbor to slide the electric beast into the slot under the vent where the pot-bellied stove now sat. They'd plug it in. It'd make life easier for her—at least until she'd recovered from the baby. Mom had refused, insisting their growing family would need the extra charges in the pump once the baby came.

Dad also wished Mom to use the sink water, too, but that service cost bricks—bricks Dad would work weeks to get and the family would burn through in a day if they weren't smart about it. Fletcher was perfectly able-bodied and more than willing to fetch as much water as Mom needed to cook and scrub up. Though he did so slowly.

The dishwasher, likewise, remained off and unplugged lest the tiny green light on the front suck its weight in precious electric allotment.

So Mom peeled and scrubbed and filled the house with smoke from the kindling and steam from the crocks of stew on the cast iron stove that Dad had dug out of an old antique store on the edge of the Shades and the town.

Fletcher had gone that day, years ago. Dad and a neighbor man had loaded the heavy cookstove on the back of a truck—another rare treat, riding in a vehicle. Fletcher explored the store while the men worked. Abandoned by its owners and mostly stripped of anything useful, the stove had been a rare find, buried under mounds and mounds of holiday decorations. Bulbs and greenery—the kind that doesn't go brown. Fake trees and plastic snowmen toppled out of the way of Dad and the neighbors as they worked to free up the stove.

Fletcher had latched onto a strand of electric tree lights, all white, and Dad had let him keep them—so long as he promised to never plug them in. Fletcher had draped the lights around his neck and pretended each tiny bulb was lit, twinkling bright and chasing the dark and the terrors that lurked there away.

Fletcher, a year later and terrified out of his mind at the howling of the wind in the pitch-black night, broke his promise. He plugged them in. The terror left. The lights twinkled and cast soft shadows across his small room.

Then Dad taught Fletcher a lesson more terrifying than the

night's dark. No Shader in their right mind—maybe not even most Towners—would dare plug something so vain as Christmas lights into a socket. What a waste of bricks.

Then Dad had cut the end off, leaving Fletcher with a strand of white lights, twinkling only in his memory, and a useless severed plug. It'd taken Fletcher weeks to get over the loss. But in the end, he'd grown to understand why Dad had treated him so harshly.

And in the end, with Mom's excellent schooling and sourcing of books, unknown to his parents, Fletcher had taught himself enough about wiring to strip and twist and tape back together his precious strand of Christmas lights.

But he'd not plugged them in.

Not yet.

He'd grown used to dealing with his night terrors. But Faith... Faith may need them some day. Someday soon.

Fletcher laid out three plates and silverware. Slowly. He remembered how the ladies on either side of their family had used that stove for their own many times when their bricks ran low, filling the Mayfields' home with aromas of roasts and cakes and soups that would go to someone else's dinner table.

Fletcher had been angry with the neighbors, thinking them taking advantage of his family's time and space. Fixing so much food that someone had to be planning on puttin' on. Planning a trip to CellLite for extra bricks.

Dad said not to be silly. That all the devious-minded ones are in the town, wasting bricks and doing a disastrous job managing SoLar— and CellLite's—limited resources. He'd reassured Fletcher that their neighbors in the Shades were good people. People keen on conservation and sacrificing to help one another.

And pointed out they'd brought their own kindling.

Most of those families had since found their own woodstoves—or at least engineered their existing electric ones to handle a small kindling fire, serving double duty in the wintertime as a heat source.

The front door opened. Daddy snaked out of his coveralls, trying his best to keep the SoLar particles in the entryway. Another job for Fletcher after dinner. He looked at his fingers. Destined one day to follow in Dad's steps all the way to SoLar, the pads of his digits sported thin rough spots from simply cleaning up the entry of their home and hauling water. What would they look like after a few years on the line at SoLar? Probably like his dad's. Callouses deep and rough enough to scrub Mom's cooking skillets.

"Smells good."

"Not much tonight. Same as last night." Mom laid Faith in her crib in the corner of the living room and came to the table.

Dad bent and kissed each of his ladies on their heads. He clasped Fletchers shoulder. "Smelled good last night, too."

Dad and Fletcher had hung heavy blankets and canvas drop cloths over the doorways and stair well, trapping the heat in the main living space. Their house, upscale in its day, had four bedrooms, an office, and three bathrooms. Wasted heat drainers. They hunkered mostly in the kitchen and living room. Fletcher had a bed in the office with a window facing east. That helped. Having those first rays of morning chase away the night's terrors.

When Faith was older, the siblings were to share that room.

Unless they went the way of the Canadian geese and found warmer shelter.

The family gathered around the table. They listened as Dad made small talk about SoLar and his co-workers' plights to save bricks. How CellLite supplied SoLar with the fuel to supplement the energy from the main factory's massive solar panels. Fuel harvested from the very people SoLar was supposed to serve—but never listened to.

But, in the end, what are the people to do? It was a vicious relationship. Dad was losing mass by the month. The walk to and from the factory. The physical demands. The worry over Mom and Faith. He'd lost most of his appetite and it showed in his cheekbones and hips. He'd taken to tying a length of twine through his belt loops to keep his pants up.

Dad caught Fletcher staring at him. "You okay, Son?"

"Yes." Fletcher took a bite of potato casserole, the onions and spinach wouldn't do much to help him with the puttin' on, but every little bite would help.

Mom took his face in her hands, forcing him to put his fork down. She'd not done this to him since she'd told him he was about to be a brother, though Fletcher doubted that was the case tonight. She angled his head this way and that, examining him as if deciding whether to toss him back in the pond like a bad catch or cook him for dinner.

"Are you sure you're feelin' fine? You've been slowing down and very quiet."

Fletcher pulled away, trying not to show disrespect with the distance. "I'm fine, Mom."

Dad looked closer as he chewed a bite of casserole. "You upset with Faith? I remember when I got a brother and then a sister. I wasn't too pleased with the additions—"

Fletcher shook his head. "No. I love her. I'd do anything for her." He shifted in his seat, resisting the urge to unbutton his pants. Standing was okay. Sitting pressed the waistband into his gut more by the day.

Mom sat back hard in her chair, a knowing racing across her face. "Oh, no. Fletcher. You're puttin' on."

Dad put down his fork. "No, you're not."

Fletcher's stomach churned. He'd kept his secret for months. They were bound to figure it out with his upcoming birthday, but he'd hoped to delay it for another week. Until the actual day he was old enough to walk into CellLite as a ten-year-old, sit in the chair at the front door and exit on the other side with enough bricks to help Faith through the dark nights.

"I'll be old enough next week." Fletcher sat straight up and faced his dad. Like a man. Like he'd seen his Dad do with government people and managers at the factory. Straight, direct, but respectful.

"But why? Why risk yourself like that?" Tears ran down Mom's face. She pushed her plate away.

"Because of Faith. We may need the extras. I want to be a good bro—"

"But you are a good brother. Helping. Working around here and keeping an eye on things while I'm at work."

"My mind's made up."

The top rim of the sun had sunk away. Dusk was fading fast. The family sat in near-dark over nearly cold casserole. Faith started to stir. Like the weight of the night was pressing on her tiny chest. Fletcher went to her, swaddled her tight in the green blanket, and brought her back to the table and sat—after he wrestled his pants button undone. He could barely see her eyes glisten in the dark. Tears matching her mother's formed and fell down her soft cheeks.

"I know. I know," Fletcher whispered to the baby. She paused her fussing and reached up for his face with that rogue fist. Dad plugged in a small night light near the dining room table. A portion of a precious brick to pay to get through the meal. The crystal-like star shape on top of the light unit outlet cast lonely lines of light up the walls and over their faces.

"As soon as I'm ten, we'll get through the dark together, little Faith. I've made you something special with wire and bulbs. Made it before you were even born. And we'll hang it above your crib. And we'll plug it in. And we'll have extra bricks and twinkly lights like the stars to sing you to sleep under until the sun comes up and you're not scared anymore. Just a few more nights, little sis. A few more nights."

Faith nestled against Fletcher's shirt and draped her skinny arm over her eyes as Fletcher started to hum and rock. She fussed a little, but she was relaxed. More so than the night before when Fletcher'd been sent to scrub dinner dishes in the pitch-black kitchen and she'd screamed in Mom's arms and would have nothing to do with Dad's walking her about the dark living room. She'd likely start screaming again when the nightlight had to be unplugged and returned to its lonely spot on the windowsill by the table.

Fletcher understood all too well. It was only his age and a bit of pride that kept him from having his own meltdown each evening. When the sun dipped. When even the squirrels and geese had sense to hide themselves in trembling curls of tails and feathers. When the dusk disappeared into the black hole and even the faint light wasting out from windows of far distant Towners failed to reach the edges of the Shades.

He controlled himself. Swallowed the fear deep. Lest he be known as the only boy in the Shades terrified of the dark...

Fletcher ventured a look up at his parents. Both teary, the wet glistened on their faces. Dad pushed his plate toward his son. Mom did the same. With his free hand, he dug his fork into their portions of potato casserole.

For a bit more puttin' on.

For the fuel to power a twisted strand of twinkle lights. To push the dark into the shade.

For Faith.

TEST PLOT

All she wanted was picture-perfect peace and quiet. Not likely...

As soon as I aimed my SUV off the interstate, so weary of cars jostling for one semi-truck trailer length closer to their destination for the last forty miles, I rolled down the windows, opened the sunroof, and blasted country music. I never listen to country. Not anymore.

But the genre fit the setting—and because that's all the radio picks up off exit 253. One station. All country. All the time. And I swear it's still old Charlie's gravelly voice, a familiar teenhood figure of mine, that's DJ-ing it up from the tiny two-story brick pod in the middle of our 'burg.

I relaxed back into the seat and work a cramp out of my left leg and my neck. I need a pit stop, but I've got plenty of gas and, now that there's no such thing as traffic, I can appreciate the surroundings and hang on until I reach the house.

And a pit stop now meant Deke's old gas station where you have to go in and ask for a key, go back outside to the one-seater, and hope the attendant remembered the place even had a restroom and that it had been cleaned in the last five weeks.

Mostly it never got cleaned. I imagined it was still the same.

Fresh air tinted with a hint of cut grass blew my hair into my eyes and tangles around my sunglasses. I should've taken the time to pull it back before rolling down the windows. The greens and blues and openness stretched forever into the horizon. I fill my lungs with home-grown oxygen and felt free. Man, had I missed the elbow room.

I'd grown up like this—free as a country bird—for a majority of my childhood. Circumstances and opportunities of the adulthood variety came along and pushed me north to the city where I traded horizontal grids of green fields and white farmhouses for vertical grids of brick and steel condos and businesses stacked tightly against and on top of each other.

I'd forgotten the deep breathing openness affords. Ground views extending to the fine line where land meets sky, only obstructed by parades of trees and barns and not concrete and walls of shiny glass office buildings.

I passed the airport. It was bustling. I'd never seen it this way before except that one Father's Day when they had the fly-in. Every owner of an ultralight aircraft with two to four seats offered rides to the dads. And they grilled out home-grown beef burgers.

My dad did that once. Took a ride in an ultralight. He said he'd never do it again as long as he lived. He kept that promise, if for no other reason than he'd only lived another three months after the blue and green two-seater skidded to a stop and he got out and puked in the grass next to the hangar. Mom and I'd thought he'd enjoy the flight.

We'd been wrong.

But the third annual Leinburg Father's Fly turned out to be the last annual anything the bitty town had. That was the year after Dad's ride. After that horrid crash. All the locals thought the airport would close, but it didn't. Slowly the ultralight owners and recreational flyers braved the blue Buckeye skies once more.

The airport is a small one. Mostly recreational ultralights and the occasional crop duster. If anything bigger than a ten-seater ever needed to land here, the farm butting against the end of the runway would lose a majority of its yield and two small silos.

What was going on at the runway today, I don't know.

A pang of sadness welled up. I knew it would come back, being home again. I'd prepared myself for it. I took a swig from my sweaty water bottle and swallowed the emotion. Breathed deeply. Kept driving. Tried not to imagine my father in one of the ultralight planes swooping in and out of sight behind tree clusters. Arriving, taking off. The hums of their engines waxed and waned through the open sunroof.

I imagined instead that the pilots' passengers were recording sweeping aerial views, like the ones Hollywood uses to establish beginning scenes in a film of a familiar skyline or landscape, say the skyscrapers of Chicago or the curves and ridges of the Grand Canyon.

But here, the establishing shots consist of gently rolling farmland, a lush checkerboard in hues of mid-summer greens with just a square or two of wheat gold to break up the monotony. Lines of treetops, full and equally lush, their branches reaching out in all directions for every drop of Ohio sunshine they can get. The occasional winding waterway—not bright blue like the Caribbean, but a dark, shallow gray from the air, almost mistaken for roadways save for their hairpin loops around the edges of the fields. Rooftops of farmhouses and barns and metal silo tops give way to tiny clusters of civilization with right-angled intersecting streets. Clusters of homes tucked around a single stoplight, a microscopic convenience store/gas station duo as evidenced by mini square pumps and equally microscopic parking lots.

Those clusters give way to more farmland and fields and the occasional green plot dotted with white and gray squares of the few-and-far-between resting places of old farmers, their wives, and the family lineages of the decades. I wonder if any of them could pick out my dad's plot.

As I passed the graveyard, I wondered how many people Lein-burg had lost in the last five years. Lots of plots were freshly over-turned. Mounds hadn't quite sunk in yet. I spotted four freshly dug spots.

I drove another three miles to reach the house and pulled into the black-tarred drive. Long and winding. Rose of Sharon bushes with mixed blossoms guard the end of the drive—each bush carried all shades of pinks, purples, and whites. I'd always liked those bushes. My mother planted a line of them at our property when I was a kid to mark the burial plots for beloved pets—two Boston Terriers, a box turtle, and a half-dead rabbit I'd failed at nursing back to health.

Our bushes only grew purple blooms, though. I'd not seen the hybrid colors before.

I parked the SUV on the pad under the basketball goal. Phil told me I could use the first bay of the four-car garage, but I didn't want to fool with the opener.

I stepped out of the vehicle for the first time in three hours and dug the key from the bottom of my purse. I stretched again, relieving angry knots in my neck and lower back and attempted to tame my wind-blown mess of hair.

Maxwell was already barking his fool head off from inside the house. I hoped he remembered me from the big-city visit the Websters took to come see me a couple of years back. Small as he is, I'd rather not deal with a dog bite or moody canine. I wanted to relax a little. Unwind from the congestion of the city.

Get some reading in—a novelty I'd not been afforded of late, with briefs and proofs and keeping the lawyers in my firm in line. Without paralegals, they'd be blind, deaf and dumb.

Phil had called weeks ago to ask me about housesitting, and I was all too eager to accept. They didn't want to board Maxwell, and they'd added a "garage cat" to their family to help with the mouse population. But that four-legged mooch decided not to be a mouser, so little miss Moppins had a feeding schedule, as well.

"Hey, thanks for doing this, Jessica. Just let the dog out a few times. Feed him when you eat. Feed the cat once a day," Phil had droned on with other minor responsibilities. "Don't worry about locking the garage. The farmer down the road stores some of his equipment in there and we just leave it open. That's where Moppins stays, too."

I smiled as he told me this. Midwest hospitality all the way. Unlocked doors. Sharing garages. The "Here, come stay in my house even though we've not spoken for two years" treatment.

I could've developed some really bad big-city habits as far as Phil and Anita knew. The kind my mother was afraid I'd fall into when I'd left the safety of the countryside. Took up heroin. Stealing to support a gambling addiction. Prostitution.

For that matter, Phil and Anita could be into something fishy. None of us would ever know since the only contact we'd had after I'd fled Leinburg were likes and smiley faces on one another's public-facing Facebook photos.

And everyone knows those never tell the entire story.

Anita had mailed me their house key the week before along with a lengthy list of to-do's and household appliance directions, a gas card, and a hand-written gift certificate from the only food establishment in twenty miles—KayKay's Korner. And yes, KayKay's still catered. In case I needed to know that.

I fumbled with the deadbolt. Maxwell scooted down the entryway hall, tail tucked, head lowered, and toenails skidding on the tile floor. I held my breath. Then, almost as quickly, the curly black Cocker had a lightbulb moment. I don't know if it was by scent, sound or sight, but little Max greeted me with pink tongue and wagging tail. Then he bolted between my legs, out the door, and relieved himself five feet from the sidewalk. I'd have to remember his preferred spots lest I drag dog crap into the house or onto my floorboards.

While he tended to business, I caught a quick glimpse of the fattest feline I'd ever seen just before she scurried into the side door of the garage. Moppins. All the best. I'm not that great with cats. I think they sense I'm a dog person.

The dog bumped into my legs a few more times in between exploring grass blades. The corn a hundred yards past the barn swayed in unison when the breeze kicked up. Strange, though. Every hundred feet, the line of corn was broken by wide paths of unplanted, brown ground. Square signs on tall metal posts marked the edge of each brown path. I shaded my eyes with my hands and squinted to read them. Each sign had a green emblem of some sort, I couldn't quite see from my distance, and an alphanumeric code: TP103, TP104, TP105. All the way up to TP112, then the horizon swallowed my view.

Maxwell bumped into my shins again, twisting and turning for attention. We went into the house. After pats and more wags, Maxwell settled down. I topped off his water bowl—a high-end fancy thing that filtered tap water for the most pampered of pooches—and threw him a milk bone. He scampered off to his dog bed under Phil's desk in the corner of the living room. I retrieved my lightly packed clothes bag and my laptop shoulder bag—stuffed with novels instead of my laptop. I packed more to read than to wear.

Because I'd planned on going nowhere during this house-sitting gig.

I'd planned on thoroughly immersing myself in Anita's Better-Homes-and-Gardens abode in the peace and quiet of nowhere Ohio. Just me, Maxell—and maybe Moppins—lounging on the back porch, sweaty iced beverage clinking in one hand, crisp mystery book in the other.

This. This was a Hollywood-worthy opening shot. And the first few beats played out as expected.

Everyone on cue. Dog. Obese cat. Cicadas humming their shrill summer songs in the treetops. Blue sky dotted with fat, jolly clouds. The occasional ultralight buzzing overhead to add interest.

But Hollywood enjoys shooting scenes of normality at the beginning of horror movies—right after those gorgeous aerial establishing shots. Everyone going about their usual business. Maybe dropping some clues as to what's to come—as if those of us sitting in the theater didn't already watch the trailer for this flick and know good and well what's gonna happen. Some girl will run outside in the dark. Or descend the basement steps. In nothing but bra and panties.

And the flashlights never work.

And the cell phone's battery is toast.

We all know what's gonna happen to our scantily dressed actress.

But first, the producers show us the "everyday" shot. Sunny, bright. Maybe our gal's cooking breakfast. Getting kids off to school. Grabbing the newspaper from the front porch and scanning the quaint suburb, waving hello to the next-door neighbor as she also goes about her sunny everyday routine.

Or maybe our gal's settled under the pergola in the back yard on an extra-thick striped turquoise cushioned lawn chair, iced-tea in one hand, unread novel in the other, letting the cares of city life and corporate takeovers and elbow-to-elbow people drift away with each turn of the page. Contented pooch sprawled in the grass soaking up the warm rays. Fat cat resting out of sight in the garage. Bobbing ultralights, swooping and swirling, wings tilted toward waving corn stalks and toward Phil and Anita Webster's catalog-perfect country home.

I DON'T KNOW HOW LONG MAXWELL AND I HAD ENJOYED THE afternoon outside. I wasn't as far into my book as I thought I'd be, and I'd given up on it to just be still. My iced tea was gone, ice cubes melted and diluting the remaining flavor. My eyes drifted to the skyline and corn rows numerous times. Once in a while, Max would bring me a well-worn frisbee or ball and we'd play fetch. The ultralights continued their clear-weather flying. So low sometimes that the tips of the corn may have been giving them the finger instead of peaceful waves.

I swung my legs to either side of the ottoman and readied myself to stand. I'd toyed with my phone a couple of times. I should call Mom, let her know I'd arrived safely and that I'd planned on seeing her tomorrow. Maybe meet at KayKay's. My treat since I had the certificate from Anita. But I hadn't dialed the phone yet.

I was enjoying the peace and quiet too much to give audience to her intrusive opinions and chattering gossip.

I called for Maxwell and stood up, gathered my book and drinking glass, took two steps toward the door when the ear-piercing shriek caused me to jump, dropping the glass to the patio's concrete. A plane hummed overhead, swooping above the rooftop, and I figured the noise was an engine issue. I watched as the white plane with green stripes dove and rose like a rollercoaster cart on an invisible track.

I edged Maxwell into the house around the shards of glass and grabbed a broom and dustpan from the entryway. I left the dog inside while I swept. As I brushed the last of the glass into the pan, it happened again. But this time, the plane was nowhere to be seen, its engine humming off in the distance.

Another cry.

Shrieking. Not human. Not an engine.

I froze and held my breath, hand tightening around the broom's handle as I brought the bristled end over my head. Like I'd actually ward off whatever was making that noise with a dollar store cleaning implement.

It was coming from the garage. Something was eating their cat.

I laid the dustpan full of glass on the ottoman and approached the garage where I'd seen Moppins retreat when I'd arrived.

The four-car structure was dark and my eyes weren't adjusting from the bright blue. Phil had said they leave the side door open for the cat and the neighbor. And god-only-knows what else.

I fumbled along the inside edge of the door for a light switch and after gaining a splinter for my efforts, finally met with the switch. A fluorescent hum echoed in the rafters as the lights woke up. I was standing near a tractor. A newer one, not one of the open-aired deals I'd encountered on the way here with the waving, happy farmers. This one was massive, enclosed with glass cab. Wheels almost as tall as me.

I heard another non-human moan. Not as loud as the first few shrieks.

"Hello? Who's in here. I'm house-sitting for the Websters." As each word fell out of my mouth, I felt utterly ridiculous. I knew no one was in here. I was talking to the cat—or whatever was eating the cat.

I caught movement on the other side of the tractor, in the back where Phil stored bikes and garden tools. Anita had said they feed Moppins back here. They keep her food up high so Maxwell wouldn't find it should he venture into the garage.

A couple of small, yellow orbs glowed from the shadow behind a wheelbarrow.

"Moppins? Kitty kitty. Was that you?" I still clutched the broom. I didn't think I'd smack their cat with it, but if it was rabid or something...

The cat meowed a high-pitched greeting. I crouched to get a better view. She inched toward me, taking a few steps then laying on her side and panting. I didn't know cats panted.

She was huge.

Then it hit me.

She's not fat. She's pregnant. I laid down the broom and without touching her I inspected her rear. She seemed to know I was catching on, probably insulting my stupidity in her superior feline brain at this point, but she didn't run from me.

"I've no earthly clue what to do now."

She meowed that she knew I had no clue and waddle-flopped-waddle-flopped out the side door and toward the house. My phone was still on the patio. I hated to bother the Websters on their vacation, but they should've included this minor detail in their long list of information.

I followed Moppins from a distance. I'd have to make that call to Mom tonight. I had no idea if she'd know what to do either, but maybe she'd know who could help.

Moppins finally reached the edge of the pergola. She inched behind a Rose of Sharon with its pinks and whites and purples and nestled into the mulch. Another faint cry and she started grooming between her legs.

As I picked up the phone to call my mother, it rang.

Anita.

Thank God.

She and Phil made it safely to Myrtle Beach. Great. Good for them.

"By the way, I think your cat's in labor."

A pause on the other end.

"Hello, 'Nita? What do I do?"

A rustle. Phil came on. "Hey, Jessica. She's a barn kitty. Country cat. She'll handle things herself."

"Yeah, but does she need water or towels or—"

"Come to think of it, why don't you boil some water, call the midwife, and ready the umbilical clamps." He laughed.

That ticked me off. "I know I grew up here, but we didn't deal with this kind of stuff." People hear you grew up in the country and they all think you know how to run a farm. Shear sheep. Milk cows and goats and birth kittens. But you don't. I don't. Our country home was just that. Country. Not farm.

Dad was a businessman. Mom drug us out here. I swallow another lump rising in my throat.

"Funny, Phil. Really, she's by the house now."

"She'll likely have the kittens and move them back to the garage. It happens all the time."

"All the time?" The poor creature looked at me with here-we-go-again eyes. "Why don't you have her fixed?"

Another pause.

"We haven't gotten around to it. She's a pro. It'll be okay. Just make sure she has fresh food and water out in the garage away from Maxwell's reach. And don't let him eat the kittens."

My gut knotted up. All my earlier relaxing washed away with a screaming cat in labor. This was not what I'd signed up for.

After a touch of small talk and them assuring me to make myself at home a dozen times, we hung up. I stood with hands on hips and watched as Moppins licked herself and then rested into the mulch. When she laid still, I watched as the little ones moved inside her, her tabby stripes rippling like the rows of corn.

I gathered the dustpan from the ottoman and dumped it inside the house. I filled a plastic bowl with fresh water and took it back outside to Moppins, setting it on the concrete near her head, just in case she needed it.

I put Maxwell on the leash—so he wouldn't bother the cat—and took him for one last walk around the edge of the yard out toward the crops. The setting sun was tickling the tops of the corn and lightning bugs floated up from the grass. I walked a few feet into one of those brown paths between the corn. The emblem on the sign was an inverted green and white striped triangle. In tiny red lettering above the solid black TP105, it read "TEST PLOT ONLY." As I tried to process this, another shriek from Moppins barreled across the yard and beckoned me back to the house. Maxwell looked up at me with coal-black eyes. "It'll be a long night, buddy." He pulled toward home.

I wondered how many cats the Websters would own come sunrise.

I COULDN'T SLEEP. WHEN MOPPINS' VOCALIZATIONS REACHED beyond the sliding glass doors onto the couch in the family room where I'd decided to make my bed for the night, I worried about her.

When I didn't hear her, I worried about her.

And I don't even like cats.

I'd left the porch light on and peeked out the curtains multiple times. I could still see her fat body nestled behind the bush. She'd not touched the water.

Back and forth from the couch to the window. Maxwell watched my struggles from his curled-up position in Phil's recliner.

I finally gave up on sleeping altogether and made an executive decision. I'd bring Moppins into the family room just for tonight. So some other animal didn't hear her cries—or the cries of her babies— and come barreling out of the field or from behind the garage and devour them all whole.

Cleaning up broken glass was one thing. Cleaning up a kitty massacre was quite another.

I rummaged in the utility closet and found an older looking plastic tote. No easy task given Anita's propensity for all things fine and functional. I lined the tote with towels from a bin marked "Maxwell's Muddy Feet." He watched me with dog-like curiosity and cocked head when I stole his toe towels. "I'll wash them and put them back."

He didn't think so.

"Or I'll buy you new ones."

I gave him the play-by-play of my plan. "And you, Sir Max, will be kind and stay away from her, right?"

Phil had said he didn't bother the cat. But that was outside. This was Moppins on his inside turf.

I readied another bowl of water—though I have no idea why—extra towels, a trash bag and some rolls of paper towel next to the tote on the family room floor. I locked Maxwell in the bathroom with another milk bone. If Phil knew what I was about to do...

I pushed the thought aside, grabbed a towel, and slid open the patio door. The porch light's rays reached only a couple of feet beyond the pergola. The garage had some safety lights around, but beyond that nothing but darkness. I knew the corn was out there, but the darkness gobbled it up. Even the lightning bugs had given up their dance and went to bed.

Moppins stirred a little bit. I shone the light from my cell phone around in the mulch and around all the bushes. I didn't see any babies. "No progress, yet, huh?" I bent to her level and draped the towel over her body. She didn't move. A faint meow.

"I'm gonna pick you up now. Don't slice me, okay?"

Another meow, and as I reached for her, I heard a howl and barking from beyond the corn. She jumped and gave a painful moan. I jumped and then froze. "Please don't slice me. We've got to hurry."

The skin on the back of my neck bristled. And I imagined, if she were spry with an empty womb, her back would've arched and her tail would've bushed out at the sound of the predator coming toward us in the midnight black.

I tucked the edges of the towel under her body and scooped her up, praying the whole time I wasn't causing her pain and that she'd not cause me any blood loss.

I fumbled into the house and got her into the tote, turned and slammed the sliding door shut and locked it. I killed the porch light, as if that would keep whatever howling fanged thing away, and tucked the long linen curtain against the wood trim.

I pulled back the towel and inspected the cat. She didn't seem to mind the tote. At least I could see her and know what was going on this way. I dimmed the lights and got Maxwell out of the bathroom and attached his leash to his collar.

I led him to where Moppins rested. Her little birthing corner Max and I had set up. I let him see inside the tote. Moppins and the Cocker touched noses. "Be good. Or I'll lock you back in the bathroom."

I swear that dog gave me an eye-roll before stretching out lengthwise against the tote. Moppins laid her head down on the Maxwell's clean "muddy feet" towel and both animals seemed content with each other's company. I breathed out a much-too-long-held breath and took off Max's leash.

The whitewashed wooden mantel clock—a clock nearly as big as that tractor's tires—ticked off one long second after another. It was only one a.m.

I felt like I'd been birthing cats for days.

And I don't even like cats.

A COUPLE OF SNOOZES AND SEVERAL FITFUL HOURS LATER—FOR me and the critters—and the Websters were two cats richer. I'd missed both of the kittens coming into the world, either from a quick rest in the recliner with Maxwell or when I was so restless I'd decided to water the house plants—and Anita had dozens of pots—a whole day early in the middle of the night.

But I could see tiny tails and wriggles in the towels near

Moppins' furry belly. I didn't touch or maneuver the momma away from her babies. I decided to trust Phil on this one and let Moppins do her thing.

Daylight trickled under the sliding glass door's drapes, and I let Maxwell outside after a cursory visual sweep of the backyard.

No jackals.

No hyenas.

No howling, rabid coyotes waiting for a snack of domestic pets.

I threw another one of Max's towels over my shoulder and picked up the tote. The smell coming from the "birthing" corner was a little rancid, so I figured it was safe to move the mom and new ones to the back of the garage. Save Moppins the trouble of transporting at least two—maybe more by end of the morning, as her belly was still swollen in my unexperienced opinion—all the way across the yard one drooping baby at a time.

I left the sliding glass door open to help the family room air out. The morning was cool, humidity free and a glorious breeze sent the linen drapes dancing across the hardwood.

I grabbed the tote of kitties and headed for the garage. Moppins blinked in the brighter daylight and curled back against the towel and her newborns. I caught a glimpse of one baby. Well, half the baby. The front half. Blind and searching with nose up for a meal. I think.

I don't know much about cats.

I fumbled to get the lights on again and took the family to the back of the garage near the wheelbarrow. I laid the clean towel next to the tote and carefully tilted the plastic container at a 45-degree angle using a couple of loose paving bricks I found in the back. Moppins adjusted and seemed to understand the plan. She'd likely move the babies out of the tote on her own and I'd not have to get my human-y germs all over her babies.

"Long night gal. I wish you the best." I saluted her. Don't know why. I filled her food bowl with fresh kibbles and topped off her water dish. Maxwell came into the garage barking.

"Oh, no. Let's go." I pointed to the door we came in, but the dog was curious about the new goings-on in the back of the garage. "Maxwell, I said come." He nosed Moppins gently, but she gave him a protective mother swat across his snout. He yelped and backed up, ran in front of the tractor where he clanged around on something. I followed him.

"Listen, you've got to leave them alone. She'll blind you good, buddy." Max had bolted to the front of the massive tractor and knocked into a pile of metal in the back of the garage.

Fence stakes.

Or signposts.

Like the ones marking the edges of the brown pathways in the field behind the garage. I bent down to straighten the mess. Max had knocked over a dozen posts from a neat stack. Dozens of stacks lined the back wall. I stacked the loose ones like the others.

Maxwell had tucked himself under a heavy canvas tarp near the poles. I lifted the edge to find the wary Cocker backed up against stacks of signs. The rectangles that attach to the tops of the poles. All with those inverted triangles. I lifted the tarp a little further as Max ran behind me. All TP90's in one pile. A stack of TP80s, running the whole range of numbers. Some signs had green checks at the top right corners. Others had huge red Xs through the entire sign.

A dozen neatly arranged piles under the heavy canvas. Likely belonged to the farmer who shared this barn. The one who owned the tractor.

I replaced the dusty tarp and called for Max again. That same prickle of fear that plagued my neck skin last night came back. Don't know why, though. Maybe the thought of a spider or other critter lunging from under the covering or from under some pile of farm junk had me on edge. Or the lack of sleep.

One more quick check on Moppins and I said, "Let's get out of here, Max."

I killed the lights and called my mother.

THE ONLY DIFFERENCE IN KAYKAY'S DINER TODAY AND FROM the last time I visited the establishment eight years ago was the layer of grease that seemed to hang in the air and on the chrome-trimmed tabletops. The menus hadn't changed. Poorly made copies laminated —more than likely by Kay herself in her spare time—boasted all-you-could-eat biscuits and gravy.

That's what I ordered. With water. Because I planned on napping later and didn't need the jolt of caffeine.

Mom ordered the same with black coffee.

"So why'd you come back?" Mom twisted and turned the steaming mug in her hands. She'd barely looked at me. Not the reception I was anticipating. I was readied for a fight, but not from this stance.

"Well, Phil and Anita—"

"The Websters?" Her eyes widened. She took a sip of her coffee. I took a sip of my water. An ultralight—we're five miles closer to the airport at Kay's than at the Websters' home—buzzed overhead and the engine noise vibrated the front window panes.

Someone in the back dropped a tray. Kay let out her all-time famous string of curses from behind the swinging wooden partition that divided the dining area from the kitchen. Cursing the broken plates and wasted food. Cursing the planes and the airport and all the needy customers.

Some things never change.

But mother.

"Yes mother. The Websters needed a dog sitter. And their cat gave birth last night so that was fun."

She didn't say anything.

"So how have you been?" I asked. We'd Skyped a few times when the connection was good enough to handle a sustained conversation. All small talk. For the last eight years or so. "How's the house and Joey?"

"If you want to know about Joey, you should talk to Joey."

Mother had been trying to get me and my brother on speaking

terms since Dad died. He blamed me for Dad's death. Said if he'd never taken that flight, he'd not have gotten sick. And the flight was my idea. I guess in a little boy's brain, connections are not always logical. Dad got air sickness that day after the ultralight flight, then they found the cancer. One had nothing to do with the other.

I sighed. I was glad when the waitress, a skinny little thing with pale blue eyes and blond hair nearly shaved off, brought our biscuits. Mom waved her away and gave her a gentle smile. "No, sweetheart. This'll do."

Then to me she said, "Jessica, you shouldn't have come here. You should've told me you were coming and I could've told you to stay away." She dug the end of her fork into the gravy-drowned biscuit.

"What are you talking about? I thought it was high time I came home. This gave me a good reason." I choked on the words as they came out. I should've visited a long time ago. Using house-sitting as a reason to visit my childhood home sounded so trite. But Mom didn't seem to notice.

"Jess. Go back to the city. Now. I'll take care of the dog and cats. I'm serious."

"What are you talking about?" I asked again. My breakfast steamed in front of my nose, but my appetite was disappearing fast.

"I don't let Joey bring the kids. I don't let Joey come. I go to him. I'll come see you. But you should leave today." She stopped my hand before I could bring my glass of water to my mouth. "Don't drink that, either," she whispered. "Go down to Deke's and get some bottled for your trip home. But don't drink the tap."

I sat back in my booth and toyed with the fork as I studied my mother. Wrinkles had sprung up where there once had been soft, supple skin. Or maybe they'd not sprung. Maybe our Skype moments just didn't highlight them the way the natural light spilling in from Kay's plate glass did. Her eyes were paler. Bluer more than the hazel they'd once been. Her hair grayer.

"Mom, please tell me what's going on."

Her eyes moistened. She took another bite and a tear trickled down her cheek past a couple of more age spots than had been there a year ago. "Go back to your job, Jess. Back to the city. Get away from here."

I crossed my arms. I felt like a teenager again. In a standoff about the cigarettes she found in my desk drawer. About the boy I wanted to run off with. About the day I declared I really was leaving this burg for the job in the city. "I'm not leaving until you tell me why." I grabbed my ice water and took a long, exaggerated drink and set the glass down with a little more oomph than I'd meant to, startling our tiny waitress into thinking we needed refills.

Mom waved her off again. "Jessica. It's all poisoned. Every bit of it. Everyone who lives here. We all know. We've all had…problems. That's what got your dad. That's why the graveyard's filled up. That's why…" she lowered her voice as she lowered her shoulders toward the table, beckoning me to do the same. When I was as low over my biscuits as I could get without soaking my shirt in the gravy, she whispered, "…the airport is so busy. No one here leaves. We've been paid off."

She straightened.

"Mother, come on."

"Paid to stay and paid to stay quiet. How do you think Phil and Anita could afford all that stuff in that house of theirs? High end this. Best of that. Grand vacation. If the Websters were smart, they'd not come back, either."

"Mom. Really."

"Jessica. Leave. Today. And if you see them land, run. They'll make you stay." She was getting agitated and motioned our waitress for the check.

"You're not making any sense. I got this, Mom." I fished out the KayKay's certificate Anita had mailed me and handed it to the girl.

Mom was nodding. Smiling. That smile she'd gotten when she knew she'd win the argument. Half smile, half smirk. "They've left. You won't hear from them again. You were their exit strategy."

I look at my aging mother right in the face. And then it hit me.

Kind of like the realization that Moppins wasn't just fat. Mom isn't just old.

Somewhere along the line. Somewhere in the last few years it happened, easily hidden in birthday cards and Christmas videos. It was right there.

Dementia.

I sat back in the booth again and this time I tear up. First Dad with the cancer. Now this.

And later, back at the Websters, I'll have to call Joey for the first time in eight years.

When the waitress brought back a dab of change leftover from the certificate, she reached across me slightly to take away my untouched food. The collar on her button up shifted slightly and I caught sight of a port near her clavicle. One that fed chemotherapy or other such poisons into the dying.

Now the girl's hair made sense. Her weight. Similar to Dad's decline.

How sad.

The entirety of Leinburg seemed to be growing old. Even the young.

Mother and I hugged in the parking lot. A quick hug on her part, but I made the embrace last a little longer than I normally would've been comfortable with. "Mom, it'll be okay. I'll be back soon. I'll come out to the house and see you there before I go back to work Monday."

She took my face her in hands. "Jessica, you're not listening. You never listen. Leave today. Go back to the Websters'. Get your things. And leave town." An airplane bobbed above us and mom winced. "Please go." She got into the pickup truck and drove away. I'm not sure she should be behind the wheel.

I sat in my SUV and stared at the front of KayKay's. I watched as old farmers and young couples came and went in a slow trickle. The diner was busier than I'd ever seen it when I was growing up here. The same ultralight circled back around and waved a wing at the town.

And I bawled.

For my mother.

For Dad.

For the little waitress girl.

And for the lost weekend of peace I'd so desperately needed.

Maxwell greeted me whole-body, tail wagging, pink tongue flashing, wriggle butt all the way. I'd only been gone a couple of hours, and most of that spent driving around the countryside, watching the planes, observing the test plots—which were everywhere. That's what they're called. Test plots.

Deke told me.

Because as I passed old Deke's gas station to top off my tank, I decided to go inside and ask a couple of questions, not to get bottled water. Deke was working. Greeted me warmly. Asked me what I was doing back. How long I was staying.

And acted relieved when I said just for the weekend.

Or maybe the short visit with my mother had bred paranoia in me. There'd been a lawyer at my firm who'd taken family medical leave to care for his dad with Alzheimer's disease last year. When he returned, he complained that he was just as bad off as his dad some days, the caretaking of someone in such a state rubbed off on him. It took him weeks to shake off the thought that he, too, had dementia.

Deke rattled on with small talk. Weather. Tractors. Who got new ones. Who refused to cave to the tech and stayed old-school with rust buckets and gas guzzlers.

I asked him if he'd seen my mother or brother lately. Nope. Hadn't seen Joey in years. "Your mother, though. She's a tough old bird. Hangin' right in there."

"Do you think she's doing okay out here. Alone, I mean?" I tried to hold back the moisture that I thought had dried up in KayKay's parking lot.

"Doin' as well as anyone else in these parts, I suppose." And that was all I could get out of him about that.

I asked about the signs. The TPs with the numbers. I thought this was small talk. To get the topic onto something not family-related. His face sombered. His old tanned hide and deep wrinkles darkened. His voice changed. Soft and somber.

"Test plots, those are. Trying out new stuff. For the good of the country." He took a greasy, plaid handkerchief from his back pocket and wiped his brow. "Hell, for the good of the world's food supply." He waved his hand through the air like he was preaching a sermon.

Then he'd changed the subject as quickly as I'd brought it up.

And offered me a free flat of bottled water for the road. When I tried to decline, he hoisted the twenty-four pack case onto his shoulder and put it into the passenger floorboard of my SUV. He gave me a half-hug. Told me to tell my momma hello when I spoke with her next and wished me all the luck when I go back to the city.

And then I left Deke's station more confused than when I'd left Kay's.

Maxwell buzzed off behind the garage where I'd last thrown his frisbee. I broke loose a couple of the bottles from the pack of water and took them into the house. May as well.

I filled Maxwell's filtered water bowl with tap water.

Filtered water bowl.

For a dog.

Ultralights scanning the crops and skies and traffic patterns—or lack thereof. Mom and Deke.

Now I know how that lawyer felt. Dementia and paranoia are quite contagious.

Another plane hummed low over the crops as I called Maxwell inside. I wanted to check on the kittens in peace. See if Moppins had that last one or two while I was away at breakfast. Another milk bone.

At this rate, the treat box would be empty long before Phil and Anita come back.

If they come back.

I strolled out to the garage and flipped on the light. The fluorescent buzz greeted me again. As did a low moan.

Poor Moppins. Still going at it. Maybe I should call Phil again. Maybe get the name of their vet, or at least the phone number, which oddly enough, in the enormous list of things they left me notes on, was not anywhere to be found.

Moppins was out of the tote and nestled inside the empty wheelbarrow. She meowed long and low at me when she saw. I sat the tote upright and gathered the towels when I saw them.

Two tiny kittens wadded in Maxwell's toe towel. Stiff. Unmoving.

And I cried again. And I don't even like cats.

I nudged one of the bitty bodies. Cold. I turned it over with one finger, just to be sure. What greeted me sent chills and goosebumps back down my neck. More severe than the spook I'd had last night with the howling.

Then I dropped the tote and looked at Moppins, who seemed to understand. She moaned another long, low song. Sorrow-filled cries for her dead babies.

Her malformed ones that wouldn't have made it no matter how good of a mother she was.

The kitten I'd turned over had five legs.

I gathered my breath and looked under the towel in the tote. The second baby. Poor soul. Had a poorly deformed head. I must've seen just the parts that were whole this morning. I'd not seen either of their bodies entirely. They would've been little Garfield kitties. Orange and black.

Moppins, still in the wheelbarrow, shifted a bit onto her side. There, suckling at her engorged nipple was another tiny baby. This one will look like her. Gray tabby. If it lived.

Oh, god, please.

"Can I see, Moppins?" I singsong at her and rub her head with two of my fingers. Two that hadn't just touched her dead babies. She didn't seem combative or protective. Just a mourning, worn-out mother.

I reached down for the infant and nudged it this way and that. I didn't see extra appendages. I didn't see any deformities, other than the fact it was a newborn kitten and not that attractive. I gently rubbed over Moppin's belly and paused over the spot where I'd seen the kittens moving inside of her just last night. I couldn't feel anything else moving. Maybe it was over. She got one child for her efforts.

Other than emotionally worn out, she didn't seem to be in physical distress.

I gave Moppins the last clean towel I'd brought to the garage. She nestled against it inside the wheelbarrow, moving her baby gently with her. I checked her water dish.

Untouched.

I retrieved another water bottle from the SUV. I dumped her dish out right there in the garage floor and filled it, in front of her, with the bottled water. She abandoned her baby in the towel in the wheelbarrow and ran to drink. I ran my fingers along her back. She nudged against my shins, drank some more, then returned to her infant.

And the goosebumps returned to my neck.

AFTER DISPOSING OF THE BABIES IN A SHALLOW GRAVE NEXT TO the field so Maxwell wouldn't snack on them, I decided to call Phil again. I desperately wanted to leave them alone on their trip, but I thought this warranted a little warning and explanation.

I released Maxwell to the backyard. I dialed Phil as I tossed the ball for the dog. It went to voicemail. I didn't leave a message.

Same with Anita's number.

Probably at the beach. I'd have to try again when the sun goes down tonight.

If they both see that I'd called, maybe they'd get the hint and one would call me back.

A few more tosses of the ball, and Maxwell trotted past me with it to the mulch where Moppins had first laid last night. He flopped down in the shade and chewed on the slimy ball in lazy contentment.

I snuck inside to grab a protein bar, since my breakfast didn't happen, and my novel to give it another go.

As I walked past the sofa table and countertops filled with gorgeous décor and Anita's houseplants, I stopped. The plants I'd watered last night were turning brown. My heart sunk. I ran to the formal dining room. Not all, but some of the green leaves were falling off or turning brown.

Same with the fig tree in the entryway.

Panic set in.

Dead kittens and now I'd done something to the plants.

I grabbed the list of directions Anita had given me. And there it was. Plain as the nose on my face, but I'd missed it entirely.

Use only filtered water for the house plants. In my cat-in-labor stupor, I'd missed that direction and used water from the tap.

My mother's words rang back to me from the diner. The near slap of the hand when I tried to drink from the glass.

The drink I did take from the glass.

I ran to the bathroom and made myself throw up.

OVER THE NEXT FEW HOURS, I PLACED FIVE MORE CALLS EACH—and voicemails to boot—to Phil and Anita. The next-to-last calls informed me their voicemail boxes were full. The last call to each number was met with a recorded message that the numbers I dialed were no longer in service.

I scrolled for them on Facebook. Their profiles were gone. I checked the photos I'd posted of our company party for the paralegals back in January. I knew both Anita and Phil had liked and commented on the video of me and a co-worker singing karaoke that night. "Country Roads" or something like that.

Their comments were gone.

Gone. Escaped.

I was their escape plan.

I called Maxwell to me as I slid down the wall of the family room to the hard floor. The Cocker put his head in my lap, his black eyes darting back and forth from the patio door to my face.

"What now, buddy?" He shifted his weight to his belly. "What now?" I scanned the house. The garden glory, picture-perfect house. I heard the ultralights flying over again.

And I made another executive decision.

I decided to obey my mother for the first time since I was like five years old.

After gathering my things and packing them into the butt of my SUV, I searched the Websters' home for all things Maxwell. Toys, treats, dishes. Not the water dish, I'd buy him a new one. And not his toe towels, we'd run out of those during the birthing.

I boxed up his things in one of Anita's prissy fabric-covered totes.

I left a note apologizing to Phil and Anita, should they ever return, for the death of the plants and two kittens—though the babies weren't my fault. I didn't decide to live in the middle of a toxic testing lab. I also told them should they want Max back, they'd have to pick him up in the city. I'm not returning to Leinburg.

I also stole ten of their best, most fluffiest towels from the guest bathroom. I told them this, too, and decided I wasn't sorry about it.

Before I locked up the house, I emptied one of the bottles of water Deke had given me. I ripped off the label to distinguish it from the rest of the bottles. I filled it with tap water and tucked it into my bag.

I leashed the dog and put him in the back seat. He seemed excited for the opportunity to take a ride.

"Stay here. I'll be right back."

I went to the garage underneath a low-flying ultralight. Circling and dipping this way and that above the crops behind the garage. It got lower and lower. So low I could've waved to the pilot. I ignored him.

Then I remembered mom's words. *And if you see them land, run.*

I ran.

I flipped on the light and ran to the piles of signs and tossed up a corner of the tarp. I photographed what I could and didn't bother replacing the covering. I even got one of the tractor.

I stuffed the phone into my back pocket and ran to the wheelbarrow. "Hey, little momma. We gotta move again. Just a little more jostling, and you and baby will be settled." I scooped up the baby in the towel. It had curled into a tiny ball and was fast asleep. I was glad I didn't have to remove it from mealtime. That may have ended differently.

Moppins followed me as I jogged with her baby out of the garage.

Back to my SUV. Just as I saw the plane dip even lower behind the garage.

I nestled the baby in the front seat on the fluffy guest towels and patted the seat for Moppins. She got the hint, smart lady that she is, and nestled next to her sleeping infant.

I heard the engine lull then shut off.

I put the SUV into drive and skidded down the lane, wheels screeching on the asphalt and tears streaming down my face as a pilot rounded the corner by the garage where me and the cats had just come from.

I bawled all the way to the interstate where I used the 253 on-ramp to head north. Back to the city. Away from the test plots. Away from the deformities.

Away from my childhood home and my not-demented mother.

And back to the law firm where I might be able to do something about it all. To blow the whistle. I have the sample of tap water. I have the sign photos.

And I know where I buried those tiny little bodies.

Then I bawled some more.

I cried for Phil and Anita. Even though it was more for the pets' sakes than theirs.

I cried for Maxwell and the adjustment he'd have to make from the open country romps to apartment living and dog parks.

I cried for Moppins and the dead little ones and the one that may or may not make it.

When I'd gathered myself, I realized the country music station was still playing. Old Charlie's gravelly voice came on. Greeting all of Leinburg with the weather report and happy flying forecasts. I shut him off. I was afraid it'd bother Moppins.

I reached over and gave her a soft nuzzle under her chin. She blinked at me and purred and wrapped her front paws around her baby. I wiped snot on my sleeve and smiled at her.

And I don't even like cats.

EVERY 24 MINUTES

In a modern world filled with wars and tragedy, a secret organization keeps the sum total of human emotion in check with sacrificial operatives who purge humanity's passions and sentiments...every 24 minutes.

On September 11th, 2001, every satellite, computer terminal, phone line and media network on planet Earth aired the same story. They did so for weeks with an intensity that taxed communications beyond anything ever seen before.

That's why Julie King went missing two weeks later.

Julie started high school at Grove Academy in August 2001, eager to get on with her senior year along with her twin sister and move out of Cedar Grove for good. Then the 11th came and the world stood still. News of the attacks buzzed in the school halls, around dinner tables, and in the only coffee shop tucked in the back corner of the only gas station in town.

It hadn't seemed real. It hadn't sunk in. It was something that could never happen to the isolated community. The small-town folks felt safe nestled in the grove. No one knew anyone who'd died that day. No one had any real connection to the awful event.

At any length, the residents had shared and chatted and reposted pictures of the tragic sights online and in the Herald—circulation three thousand—and sent care packages. Julie and Jamie's senior class had collected teddy bears to send to the victims' families. The twins had taken a shift standing at the intersection of Central and Park under the town's one stoplight to collect funds from the drivers to purchase those bears.

It all seemed so long ago.

Now, Julie watched with contented sadness as her monitor flashed pictures of her and Jamie standing in that intersection. And then her senior picture in her volleyball uniform taken the summer prior. Next, all of them together at the lake from spring vacation that Mom had had framed and put on the fireplace mantle next to the girls' baby photos.

The camera cut to the front of her house showing three people huddled together under the red maple tree in the front yard. She could see the tips of the microphones at the bottom edge of the screen. And the lady. The lady was crying. And the gray-haired man said if anyone had information on Julie's whereabouts, could they please call the hotline, because they hadn't given up hope yet.

A younger woman, Julie's twin, with Julie's same piercing blue eyes and Julie's shade of blond stood between their parents with her arms around the couple.

Her family still missed her. But they seemed... complete.

The working theory, according to the news reporter, was that an out-of-town motorist had spotted the attractive young girls at the intersection that fateful day and had targeted Julie—or Jamie, for that matter. Jamie's boyfriend had picked her up afterward, leaving Julie to walk home alone. Julie never made it home, though.

Something entirely different had picked up Julie.

She pushed back from her workstation to stretch and look out the window. From the fifteenth floor of the Company, she had an excellent view of Ground Zero. She'd watched for years as the cleanup had waxed and waned, equipment coming and going. She'd watched the people wax and wane, too. Each September the memorial lights went up, with flowers and candles and photos. Then, a few days later, workers would come and clean it all up so life could move on. And every September, Julie took a copy of what would have been her senior photo, printed from the Herald's website, and propped it among the rest of the photos and flowers.

Because she had died that day, too.

She wasn't ungrateful or bitter. Nothing like that. She understood now what had to be done. And she understood why. She rubbed the bump under her forearm and returned to her desk.

The Company had been a great help, even though she had feared them at first. They had dealt with this type of disappearance before. In fact, the Company had mediated Henote requests for decades and had developed the tech to make the lives of the candidates easier.

The Henotes had calculated that Julie must recalibrate every twenty-four minutes. One poor soul in Japan must recalibrate every eight minutes, the Company told her. Poor soul.

Twenty-three minutes had elapsed since she'd last dosed. She opened the engraved wooden box on her desk, removed the disk and placed it on her forearm. It didn't hurt anymore and, unless someone looked closely, they would never know she had an implant.

The Company had explained that they'd planted others like her in major cities all over the world, but she could never meet them. The Henotes wouldn't allow it. They also explained she was doing it for the good of the planet, but that job seemed impossible.

Twenty-four minutes. Julie placed her index finger on the disk's scanner. Done.

Free for twenty-three minutes.

One time, about six years ago, Julie had missed the twenty-four-minute mark by thirty-two seconds. The communication system had gone down in all of New York, and ten people had died.

She hadn't missed a dose since.

It took her a while to understand that the recalibrations didn't stop bad things from happening. They stopped bad things from *spreading*. Emotions as powerful as fear and terror spread all the way to the edge of our universe and bump into the Henotes' realm, especially when those emotions are intensified en masse by tragedies like tsunamis and terrorists crashing planes into skyscrapers.

And, unknown to most of the human race, our satellite and radio signals amplify those emotional energy waves. The Henotes' very existence depends on human recalibration to disperse the negative energy and the toxic emotional waves and—

Well, she really didn't understand how it worked. Only that it did. The Henotes kept up their end of the bargain so long as Julie and others like her kept up theirs—the bargain that the Company had negotiated a hundred years ago. The bargain where the Henotes allow humans an existence so long as we don't swallow them with our feelings.

She put the disk back in the box and went back to work scanning the news footage of anything that might cause a ripple of emotion large enough to warrant another candidate. She smiled as she remembered that her biggest goal in life used to be to leave Cedar Grove. She'd certainly accomplished that one.

Her family didn't know she existed. They only knew she was gone. The Company and the Henotes gave her an existence, of sorts. Everything she needed was provided—everything but real emotional connections.

Two years ago, she'd considered suicide after she'd seen the Herald's yearly anniversary piece of her disappearance. At least her parents could have closure and she could finally rest for more than twenty-three minutes at a time. Before she could devise a plan, a 28-year-old Canadian candidate had accomplished what she was contemplating.

The Henotes replaced him with his twin brother two days later.

Her monitor beeped and an alert flashed at the bottom of her screen. A 7.5 magnitude earthquake had struck California's coast just seconds ago.

She reached for the switch above the monitor and flipped it from green to red. She typed in the coordinates of the quake and scheduled a pickup.

The Henote ship would arrive in two weeks from five seconds ago in a small, isolated town hundreds of miles from the quake. She wondered if Megan or Melissa Henry would be the new candidate.

She wished she could sit the new girl down and give some advice. She wished someone would have done that for her early on.

Saving the world? Too big. Saving her sister from a similar fate? Worth it.

Her recalibration alarm sounded. Twenty-three minutes.

One minute to go.

THE QUEST OF SOULS

Tamryn is pregnant and beside herself with joy. She and her unborn child are on their way to choose the very essence of life for her baby, crafted by the Centre's lineup of geneticists and techs and watched over by the ever-present drones. But will this Quest of Souls, a once-in-a-lifetime journey, be all that Tamryn hopes? Or will the Pool of Available Souls run dry before she reaches her destination?

Tamryn pulled her fraying shawl around her shoulders and wrapped a shaky arm around the child growing inside her. She leaned her forehead against the stainless-steel wall as the season's colors blurred outside the oval window. She was grateful for the window seat with room enough to lean on the train's frame, as unfeeling as it was. A few stolen glances around her, and others weren't so fortunate. Rows of four on either side of the eternal aisle, the other three women in each seat section had to remain stiff and straight to avoid leaning on one another.

Window seats were the best.

She'd read last week in the village diary selection of how the littles of long ago would squabble for the window seats in ancient automobiles and flying craft. How they'd make pitstops and road trips and family holidays to travel and do nothing but nothing. She couldn't fathom it.

She rubbed her stomach. Her little wouldn't be afforded that fun.

Not that the window seat on this ride was fun. She'd been escorted to this row—this seat—by a mechanical usher matching the train in every aspect. A stainless-steel shell where warm skin should be, a translucent oval flashing colors and lights where eyes should be. Unspeaking, but unmistakable in intent and direction when it pointed its jointed appendage toward the wall. Tamryn was to take the window seat. Every other woman on board whose child was due within the month also had window views. They deserved this luxury —even the Programmers thought so.

It was, after all, the Season of the Soul.

Tamryn tried to focus on the blurs whizzing by. She wished she could enjoy each hue in isolation. Red oaks. Mustard hickories. A few pines and firs refused to give over their olives and hunter greens to the demands of Mother Nature.

Rebels all, even the sun and seasons. How dare those wayward ones not bow to the will of the Centre?

Elder Moreen warned Tamryn about spending too much time

with the diaries. Of learning too many useless things. "G-girl, we're to survive. Names of trees and customs of the past and antiquated bygones have no place now." Sometimes Tamryn missed the elder's meaning behind the worsening stutter. Sometimes Tamryn felt Moreen demeaned her by calling her a g-girl. She only used that term with Tamryn, even though others asked the Elder questions even more ridiculous.

And no one else called her a girl but Moreen. Tamryn had straightened her shoulders and pressed for a reason. "Then why have the diaries at all?"

"Not to relish, for certain. To remind us of how the end came to be."

"But—" Tamryn had tried to further her argument with the Elder. Moreen raised a crooked finger to her parched lips and glared over her shoulder. Tamryn followed her gaze to the Worker who, tall and steel and unfeeling, paused the water retrieval ever so slightly, its delicate audio system programmed to pick up on such talk.

To report such violations in real time to the Centre.

The old woman had leaned in close with harsh words. "Tamryn. You'll be labeled a Dreamer." Then she softened. "If you must dream, g-girl, do so with eyes and mouth shut tight."

The Worker and Tamryn returned to their tasks, the drone dealing out water rations and Tamryn grinding herbs between stones. Herbs ground by the hands of gravid women were thought to increase natural fertility.

Tamryn had her doubts about the herbs and all things natural fertility. Not one lady on this train had a natural child. Those who were that fortunate didn't require participation in the Quest of Souls, as naturals came with everything they needed—though moderately flawed according to Centre standards. No, the unborn on the train were tube babies. A series of gene sequences architected by the brightest of minds with the greatest of intentions.

Tamryn leaned her head back on the slick plastic rest and thought about using her thin covering as a pillow, but with another glance around the train, she saw no other woman doing so. Women blessed with hair pulled their gray and white locks into tight buns and braids adorned with natural leaves and sprigs of evergreen. They didn't lean on the headrests. They'd mar their Quest adornments.

Others, those women who weren't genetically inclined to have hair, simply sat with heads held high. Some had woven leaves and twigs and bright red berries from the yew bushes into crowns. Tamryn had neither the hair nor the time to weave and adorn. She'd been too busy with the diaries. Too busy dreaming.

At any rate, no woman dared give themselves comfort on this journey. Nerves were too frayed—some with excitement and some with horror. Minds racing as fast as the train sped on its invisible magnetic force. The diaries spoke of chatty women and giggling girls on trips and in schoolhouses and shopping malls. This train was silent except for the rush of air against the car and the faint tremor in the floor from the magnets.

Silence is survival. A keynote warning speech from each village's Elder. Speech, especially woman-talk, is easily interpreted as dream speech by the Workers, and, well. They all knew what became of the Dreamers.

Tamryn startled—another sign of dreaming—as Workers began rising from their stations dotting the long aisles. From overhead bins they gathered metal cylinders—some white, some red—and began passing them to the passengers. Trays with hollows the sizes of the cylinders protruded with a unified hiss from the seatbacks. Tamryn took her set from the drone's claws and, following suit with the other women in her row, dropped the cylinders into the hollows with thudded clunks.

These must be the Quest Feast courses Elder Moreen had described. To be consumed just before arriving at the Centre. On full stomachs the women would choose their children's souls. The train was close now. Tamryn's pulse raced and her palms moistened. She wiped them on her smock, and the baby jumped. It must sense Mother's worry, even in its primitive state.

The woman next to her, not nearly as close to her delivery date as Tamryn and not as young, was all smiles under her crown of berries and red oak leaves. Her first Quest. Tamryn could smell new excitement dripping off her. The woman's hands rested on the edge of the tray, tapping impatiently, waiting for the lights above their heads to turn white, then red. The signal to begin the Feast. This was Tamryn's first Quest, as well. But her excitement leaned more toward anxiety than elatedness.

Tamryn ventured a second touch of the containers with her fingertips. The white was cold, colder than the train's steel. The red was as warm as the summer sunshine at noon—those days when the village will brim with life from this year's batch of young ones. She wanted to hold onto the red one, to take a sip of what may be inside, but Elder Moreen had prepped her and the others from their village. "Don't interrupt the ceremony. Follow the lights. Try to enjoy the time. You may not get another chance to see the Centre."

"And g-girl?" Moreen had winked at her. "Be ready for anything."

Moreen had participated in this ceremony four times. A rare occurrence. It's what made her Elder. Experience. And that she'd managed three viable offspring. Two survived and became Centre Citizens—the ultimate honor and one envied by every mother. The third one, though. Moreen had been last in line, and the available souls were few and with undesirable traits. "Scraped the bottom of the Pool, I did. But at least I scraped." That child, once weaned, had been shipped off to staff a drone camp.

At least the child had made it to the Pool. Better to staff a camp with its laborious duties than to become one of them. A drone. All human, well mostly, but with dead eyes and the unfeeling hollows of the metallic Workers.

Troublemakers, every one, eventually.

Eventually, after whatever usefulness the soulless afforded the Workers had been tapped, they had to be put down. No future offspring could come from such soulless ones. It wasn't proper. It wasn't fitting for survival.

Moreen knew that experience too well and when she spoke of it, the sparkle left her blue eyes and fell down her cheeks in saltwater. Her youngest, a male born in the same month as Tamryn twenty-some years ago—a week shy of the Quest train. Soulless. Stripped from Moreen's arms by a Worker before he was even three hours old.

Raised by the drones as one of their own. Better to scrape the Pool than deliver pre-term.

No mother wants to scrape the bottom, though Tamryn knew some on her train may, given their due dates and placement in the lineup at the Centre. No mother wanted to be at the end of the line when the Pool ran dry. Tamryn shuddered at the thought and hugged her abdomen tighter.

Tamryn's stomach growled. She rested her hands on her bump and prayed the cylinders would remain at their proper temperatures. She wanted to taste each one as intended, but the lights had yet to come on. She peeked around her neighbor to the other women in her row. All sat upright, at the ready. Still no one spoke, but they couldn't be any less anxious than she. Likely reviewing what their Elders taught them.

How to behave at the Centre.

How to operate the Pool selector.

How to be still while the genetic material that would form their children's essence was injected...

That last thought sent a slight wave of nausea into her throat, and she tried to move her mind to other issues, lest she spoil her Feast.

Elder Moreen had spent extra time with Tamryn, calming fears. "All will go well, g-girl. You'll see." And the woman would run her old hands over Tamryn's abdomen, as if wishing a soul into her child right then and there. No Quest required.

With time, Tamryn worried less about her chances to choose a soul for her unborn wee one. The trains, whizzing from all directions would meet at the Centre and empty their pregnant cargo into nice, orderly lines—those due first at the head of the line. So Tamryn and those with window seats would be fine. Those near the aisles, though. They could still miss out, even though the Centre relayed that they'd solved the shortages. The recent success in fertility numbers was a good thing—they'd even added a couple of cars to each train.

The Centre assured the villagers that running out of souls was a good problem to have.

Genetics takes time.

Generations, really, to get it right.

And how lucky that they all survived to the next Quest to see another wave of youth born to carry on humanity. And all hail the Technicians and Programmers who make it possible.

And, for this year's Quest, a fresh batch of souls with all necessary elements of survival programmed in, and, yes, even a dash of whimsy sprinkled in to harken back to the days the of the diaries.

Tamryn doubted that bit. Whimsy. Sounded like dream speech, and the Centre forbade it. But from generations past, the Centre learned to give a little. Giving a little keeps the masses in line. The powers that be had to know how badly some girls want to dream despite the Programmers doing their best to rid the twisted DNA ladder of such unnecessary survival genes.

Elder Moreen had passed on this communication sent from the Centre. Tamryn and the other pregnant ladies were hopeful. "And, it says that you'll have a whole five minutes this year. Up from two minutes over Quests past. What excitement!"

Five minutes. Five whole glorious minutes to choose the perfect combination of demeanor, work traits, and whimsey—if the Centre were to be believed—for her child. The ladies buzzed about the village, making mental lists of what to look for when their spot in the line met the doorway to the Pool. Tamryn's village neighbor had her hopes set on intelligence, stamina, and longevity. A political move. One that would fare that family well at the hands of the Centre.

But the neighbor was due a whole three months after Tamryn. Tamryn's child had a better chance at that soul combination. But the thought of sending her five-year-old *there*. To the stark white building that rose eighty stories into the sky with its sharp angles and glass and metal walls breaking up the blue and the clouds and the flightpath of the few birds that lingered. Well, Tamryn hoped for something different.

Something closer.

Which meant she'd look for passion, kindness, and humility. In hopes that her child would remain a villager. Someone to share the days and diary pages with. Someone to, well, dare she think it? Dream with. Name the trees. Enjoy the colors. Be free of drones and Workers and Centre regulations. A chance for some quiet isolation with the dear one growing inside of her.

Selfish, she knew. But kinds like that were needed to lead and ensure the wellbeing of the village women, weren't they?

Moreen forever warned her against such things. "Survive, g-girl. Survive." And the three traits Tamryn hoped to find would be in supply, but they wouldn't guarantee Tamryn's family or the village she hailed from any special graces from the Centre.

And, many times, special graces from the Centre meant survival.

The light above their heads turned bright white with a chime. Tamryn startled. A couple of the ladies in front of Tamryn did as well. She was glad she hadn't been holding the cylinder, she'd have dropped it for sure. She reached for the white container and removed its lid. She smelled the liquid. Citrus and earthy, her eyes widened. She heard a couple of gasps escape the lips of the women around her.

She brought the cylinder to her lips, the cold raising gooseflesh on her arms and neck. One slow swallow. She wanted the flavors to linger. Honey, sweet and golden. Lavender. Earthy, slightly minty. And lemon. What a treat. Tamryn hadn't enjoyed fresh citrus for ages. Not outside of the encapsulated tablets brought by the Workers, anyway.

One more swallow. She closed her eyes and imagined the refreshing liquid tracing its way down her esophagus and into her stomach. The nutrients uplifting for her and life-giving for her child.

She suppressed the urge to guzzle the whole container, gulp it down. She imagined fields described in the diaries. Fields of purple sprigs against lime green grass, blowing in the breeze. Orchards with sagging tree branches, full of the sunniest lemons.

Beehives dripping pure gold in warm afternoons...

Stop dreaming girl. Survive. Moreen's voice. Reminding her.

She jerked her eyelids open lest her imagination ooze out and become noticeable to the ladies around her. Or the Worker.

The light above changed to red with another chime as she finished sipping the last drops.

She replaced the lid on the white container and put it in the hollow. She removed the red, still as warm as when it was delivered, and inhaled the steam. She recognized the spices instantly. Herbs she'd ground for months and months now. Basil, thyme, and parsley blended into a rich, red-orange soup. Tomato? Squash?

It'd been so long since Tamryn had tasted fresh produce she wasn't sure. The Centre was going above and beyond for this year's Quest.

Tamryn brought the cylinder to her lips and was about to take that first decadent sip when a screech filled the car and she lunged forward on the slick seat, tipping most of the liquid onto her smock and shawl. Gasps and cries escaped from all directions of the train. Tamryn was glad she wasn't the only one who'd spilled the precious contents.

The screech continued and Tamryn dug her sandals into the floorboard to stay in her seat. Workers rose and walked the aisles, motioning for the women to stay put. To drink and sip. But the few women in Tamryn's view replaced their cylinders and tried to clean up their messes or help with someone else's spill. The blurs outside the window slowed and became crystal clear as the train stopped. The vibrations under Tamryn's sandals faded then ceased, the magnetic rail no longer propelling the cars forward toward the Centre.

Her oval window framed a magnificent view, one that Tamryn

would've enjoyed had she not been covered in soup and bathed in confusion. The women in her seat section strained their necks to see. Tamryn pressed herself back into the seat as far as she could to afford them the view. The tree line, bright with bursts of autumn, gave way to a clearing of browning grass. Beyond the clearing, the Centre. She'd only seen it once as a child and had thought it sharp and mean. Now, it proved to be the hope of her child's future—of all their futures.

Scared whispers muttered around her as Workers began to escort women to the exit rows. Slender snakes of smoke, that of burnt circuitry and plastic, oozed their way into the car from the seams above the meal lights. Motion outside caught her eye and she froze in her seat.

People rushing the train, approaching the gravel that covered the underground magnets. People in white headdresses down to their necks. Openings cut out for mouths. And where eyes should be, single black ovals. How could they see? Dressed in rags and linen sacks. All rushing toward the train.

Workers racing after them on clunky metal legs.

Taking them by their arms.

Pushing them to the ground.

Tearing off the headdresses to reveal bald scalps on some, tangled messes of gray or white hair on others.

But the people outnumbered the Workers, and—

A cold pinch tore her away from the window. A Worker had her by the arm, pulling her from her seat and pointing the way to the exit. To the outside. The side of the train opposite the commotion.

Away from the soulless uprising.

Tamryn supported her belly with one arm and used the other to support herself down the steps to the gravel around the track. The train still hovered midair, as if held by invisible strings from the sky. The chilliness caused her to pull her soup-soaked shawl tighter. The sun was high up. Almost noon. Almost arrival time.

Arrival time. What if the other trains arrived and Tamryn's never made it?

She'd scrape bottom.

Or worse.

Some women wept in the confusion, embracing their stomachs. Others simply stood or paced, as blank-faced as the Workers that seemed to be awaiting instructions. Hovering like the train, only their steel feet dug firmly in the gravel.

Underneath, on the other side of the train, the city side, Tamryn could see legs disappearing into mangled shoes and sandals with no proper straps. Feet that kicked at the gravel and tried to crawl under the train, stopped only by the intense force of the magnets holding the metallic beast in the air.

The feet of those that had stopped the train with their ruckus.

She'd heard of this. Of the soulless protestors. Moreen had taught that celebrations and Quests had been hindered more than once by the vagrants in decades gone by.

It ended badly. Many women missed out on their chances...those women like Tamryn who were due soon. Too soon for delays, their children born without hope and in view of the very Centre that promised to give them hope. And survival.

But nothing like this had happened in Tamryn's lifetime. Maybe not even in her mother's.

Panic surged in her chest and shot through her legs. She had to move. To pace like some of the others. She wanted to run, but she had nowhere to run to.

Toward the head of the train, some of the protestors had made their way around the front end, where the magnets hadn't activated yet. Workers tried without success to contain them all. Some protestors ran toward the tail of the train—which disappeared around a bend, and Tamryn, just a few cars from the nose, couldn't see the back end.

Couldn't see what was becoming of the women in those last cars.

Moaning echoed off the train's side, deep and mournful. Labor pains. Several women, window-seat women like Tamryn, under the stress and strain of the chaos couldn't hold their unborn at bay.

Protestors overtook the few remaining Workers. Flight craft buzzed overhead, lowering chutes to drop more drones to control the scene.

Tamryn felt a sharp pain shoot low in her abdomen and around her back, squeezing her muscles, sending electric up her spine. Lights danced in her periphery, shiny and white like the light dancing between the red oak leaves. She needed to kneel before she fell.

She didn't make it to the ground. Arms—human arms with warm skin and bulky muscles and earthy sweat—wrapped one behind her shoulders and one behind her thighs, flipping her off her feet.

From this cradled position—too fearful to fight back—she was face-to-face with a white mask. Black mesh oval over the eyes. She couldn't see the eyes. Mouth hole cut. Pink lips moving from behind the heavy linen. Forming words.

Don't be afraid.

I've got you.

Something familiar. The din of the chaos behind faded like the noise in a dream upon wakening. The moans of the other women stopped. All she could hear was the words this one spoke to her. The pain in her abdomen settled. The baby inside kicked, then it, too, quieted. Listening with Mother. Waiting.

Tamryn, against her better senses, settled into the strong arms and allowed herself to be carried toward the tree line, legs dangling at the kneecaps. One arm clung to her unborn, one arm draped around the neck of the masked face.

She couldn't see the other women. The train. The Workers. Flight craft overhead focused attention behind them now. Dropping drone loads, no doubt. She knew she should hear the chaos, but she didn't.

She heard this man's footsteps. The leaves crunching under his feet. The wind high up in the oaks and hickories and firs. Reds and mustards and olives. In isolation.

Naming the trees.

Something familiar. More words.

I've got you. No more Quests for you. No worries.

Soothing. Rhythmic words of comfort to match his footsteps.

Tamryn. They lie, g-girl.

She jerked her eyes from the sky and treetops toward his face. Her legs kicked, willing her to be free of his grasp. He obliged and stood her gently on the leaf-covered ground. Forest all around. No sight of the train. No Worker in view. A few other masked ones led other women deeper into the trees. Some crying. Some quiet.

She reached up and carefully removed his mask, fully expecting his eyes to be as black and dark as the mesh that covered them.

They weren't. They were kind and blue and sparkled in the autumn rays that reached the forest floor. Alive.

Full of soul.

Full of Moreen.

"Where are we going?" Tamryn managed after a stunned moment. He was patient while the pieces fell into place and realization took hold. The son born too soon. The so-called soulless one lost to the unfeeling drones.

His blue eyes.

G-girl.

Be ready for anything, Moreen had told her.

"Someplace safe. Away."

"But where?"

He smiled a Dreamer's smile, full and bright. Moreen's smile when the Workers had their backs turned. "Somewhere to dream with your eyes wide open."

THE FRACTURED

You may need to rethink your next trip to the caverns...

Kent Ober sat in his manmade cave and allowed dread to fuel his procrastination regarding the work left on the kitchen counter. The tiny spare bedroom of the single-wide bathed him in darkness. He'd duct-taped layers of black trash bags to the trim of the lone flimsy window months ago—then hung heavy blackout drapes, not by a proper curtain rod, but with a staple gun—over the top of the bags. Extra reinforcement should the faintest beam of light invade the eastward-facing orifice in the wall.

Eastward. He avoided this room before noon. Or he tried to.

He should've done the looming work this morning, but last night's flourish of memories drove him to down at least eight bottles of liquid therapy. So he'd retreated to the dark before the sun rose to sit and recover from the binge and the fractured turquoise eyes glaring from behind shaggy brunette bangs when he closed lids on sober eyes. He shuddered and fought the urge to dig next to the chair for another bottle.

He had been pleased to find, however, that the room was so dark so early in the morning. The temperature rose a few degrees as the trailer soaked in the rising summer sun, but the light stayed at bay.

He'd sealed the seams around the hollow core door leading to the hallway with extra black gaskets made for weatherproofing car doors. When Kent pulled the door shut, he placed a rolled-up black blanket along the bottom. Between the blanket and the worn carpet, the light, ever so faint floating down the hall from the kitchen, couldn't snake its way under the door, either.

The tattered lift recliner long ago stopped being comfortable—if it ever was. After the power cord frayed, he left the footrest in its extended position as it wasn't worth the extra effort to fight it down to submission. He swung his legs to either side of the footrest, again resisting the urge to reach down for a fresh—or not so fresh—beer. The kitchen was calling.

He gripped the armrests to help him rise from the awkward strad-dled position. The purple-red fabric that had once been the selling point for his mobility-challenged mother was now more brown than burgundy. The plush microfiber hardened from years of her dripping nutritional supplement shakes and from his more recent habit of drifting off with an unopened bottle resting in his hand. The cushion corners and arms frayed down to the stuffing with abuse and neglect. Neglect and hours upon hours of silent, black contemplation in the tiny room.

He stretched out the kinks and paused as a wave of nausea threatened to send him back to the recliner.

He knew better than to retreat. To hole up. To isolate.

He should call someone. He knew this.

He also knew he was stubborn enough not to call anyone. Ever.

Kent had taught many classes for people suffering loss. Had given his own personal testimony in tiny rooms with fluorescent lighting to people like him sitting in plastic chairs arranged in half circles. Shared and talked and encouraged and leaned on. People all suffering one horrid loss or another attempting to seek solace in someone else's grief journey.

He'd taken many classes for his own wellbeing through the years. Therapy. Counseling. Then department-mandated twelve steps. And another round of twelve more steps on his own.

The things he'd seen. The things he'd had to do as a soldier then as an active duty detective in the inner city. He'd witnessed and cleaned up the aftermath of the atrocities that one human could inflict on another.

But nothing. Nothing compared to or prepared him for that day in the cave. For the loss of innocence. For those turquoise eyes and the evil that followed.

That thing that consumed his son. That *wasn't* human.

And then people stopped listening to him. Grew tired of his X-Files-level obsession with the caves. Kent understood. He was tired of his own obsession. He would've distanced anyone in his groups who'd behaved the way Kent had. He couldn't blame them.

Vicky couldn't take his behavior and obsessions any longer, and his wife of nearly twenty years left one night five months ago with no warning. Or maybe there had been warnings and he'd simply not paid attention. Maybe it was six months ago. Time has a way of slipping away in the dark.

When the dizziness relented a bit, he took a shaky step toward the door, cursing his choices. Cursing his losses. Always with the guilt and the self-hate.

When his mom passed and left him this place, void of the distraction of caring for another human, he'd remained secluded in the single-wide in the forest. Narrow and long like a cave passage with rooms shooting off from the main vein.

The kitchen served as the visitor center, complete with concessions and electricity and the bedrooms were further in the cavern where the light barely made it to the rim of the rooms—if at all. And that pathetic recliner the stalagmite that remained in the center of his black hole soaked in silence and littered with secrets. Secluded.

He knew better. He should change that. The seclusion.

Another shaky step. His feet felt like they'd been cast in limestone.

Kent made it to the hallway and leaned against the tan paneled wall. Twelve steps toward the angry fluorescent bulb hanging over the kitchen counter. Or two steps back to the safety of the black hole and welcoming arms of his tattered friend.

Two steps require less effort than twelve.

The kitchen's duties can wait. Nothing fruitful had come from any of his research, so tending to the test tubes and vials and charts under the searing light could hold for a few more hours.

Maybe for many more hours and after many more bottles.

He aimed for the spare room's door. His foot froze in midair as panicked knocks firing in rapid succession rattled down the side of the trailer. Delivery people and Jehovah's Witnesses don't knock like that. Detectives and military and frantic family amid loss knock like that.

He took another step toward the black, ready to replace the blanket under the door and shut out and wait out whomever was disturbing his peace.

"Detective Ober. I know about Malachi."

Not the first crazy to claim a solution. Probably wanted money in exchange for a big revelation. He'd fallen for that before. Desperate. The knocks and voice did not relent. Crazy. And he knew what crazy sounded like.

"Please, I need to speak with you." A woman's voice. Desperate. Pleading. He recognized the audible anguish too. A tug of the old Kent, the one that cared to fix things, annoyed him through his hungover haze.

"I know about the caves. My daughter has the eyes."

Kent spun on his heel, dizziness seizing his vision. "What did you say?" He yelled. He knew the boom of his voice could penetrate the frail trailer walls.

"I know about the eyes." She paused her pleading and beating.

He held his breath.

Then Kent rose to open the door.

———

THIS WOMAN, FRANCIE, SAT AT THE TWO-PERSON DINETTE SET his mother had purchased at a flea market. Chrome circled the table's edge, chrome that needed scrubbed. The top of the table was worn from elbows—not his or his mother's—but someone's. Kent had imagined some happy couple or a parent-child duo who enjoyed each other's company assembling thousand-piece jigsaw puzzles or playing Yahtzee for hours on end at this tiny table.

The fog cleared from his brain and he imagined the dinette set through Francie's eyes. Old. Worn. Dirty. He'd had to dust the yellow padded chair before she sat down. He'd certainly not sat there. Not for weeks.

Maybe months.

"Drink?" He opened the fridge and gazed in, letting his head linger in the cool and relative isolation of the interior. Three beers. Four water bottles—one half drank. A near-empty ketchup bottle and two-year-old mayo and soy sauce complete the list of cold groceries Kent had in stock. He pulled out two beers and popped the top off one and handed it to Francie.

"It's ten o'clock in the morning, Detective Ober."

He shrugged and took a swig. He swapped the unopened cold beer for an unopened water bottle and she accepted with a mousy thank you. He offered her a banana, but the fruit flies protested, and she put up a slender hand in refusal.

Kent tossed the banana and its brown-spotted cohorts into the overflowing trash can.

"Sorry about the offerings."

"It's okay."

He didn't bother brushing off his seat before sitting down. He twisted the beer bottle in his fingers in front of him. He knew better. What must she think? "Tell me what you know." He huffed, shook his head and took another swig. That line, the tell-me-what-you-know line, he'd used thousands of times in the course of his investigations for the military and the police force.

He sounded nothing like that old Kent.

That Kent may as well have died in that cave four years ago.

"I've been trying to track down information. Any information at all. No doctor understands. They all say she's perfectly fine. Just a fluke. No one can tell me what happened to my Sienna. All I know is that her brown eyes are gone. The turquoise eyes are there. And she's..."

"Not...Sienna, is it? She's not Sienna anymore." The third swig of this particular bottle turned his stomach.

More likely the cramping came from this woman's news. He examined her as she paused to look around his home. Her gaze swept over the tiny open living room hooked to the tiny kitchen. He followed her eyes as they drifted over the mostly vacant living area and up toward the cobweb ridden ceiling. Brown eyes. No hint of bright blue or black shards in her irises that he could tell. Brunette hair with flecks of gold pulled back into a loose bun. One lock escaped and curled in front of her ear. Delicate lips. Light makeup. Light enough to allow her smattering of freckles to show through. Simply dressed. Or hurriedly, maybe. Pink t-shirt, ripped jeans. Tennis shoes.

Kent shifted on his chair. He must still be drunk. In another life he'd have found this lady attractive. Beautiful, even. When she looked at him what must she see? His personal hygiene had taken the same course as the housekeeping since his mother had passed.

"How long ago?"

"She was fourteen. She's seventeen now."

Malachi is eighteen. He'd been fourteen when he traveled to Cave Country for his hard-earned, end-of-the-semester trip for the well-behaved, high achieving students. An overnighter and three caves tours. Vicky, the geologist-at-heart turned college professor, had been elated when he'd earned the trip. Offered to chaperone, but Malachi wanted his space from parental influence, so she'd caved.

So to speak.

Kent imagined the guilt she'd felt for not being there. Maybe her presence would have prevented whatever happened...

"—haven't heard from Sienna in weeks. Only a random text now and then." Francie wiped her damp eyes on the shoulder of her t-shirt. He didn't have a napkin or paper towel to offer her—much less a tissue.

Malachi hadn't spoken to Kent since Vicky left. Kent was left wondering about his son's whereabouts and wellbeing. Fed or hungry? Sheltered or homeless?

Alive or dead?

A parent's worst nightmare is always the not knowing. His years on the force taught him that. Francie's state confirms it all over again.

"Did she go to Cave Country?"

A nod.

"Which cavern?"

"I don't know. She was with her dad and brother. I never got a clear answer from them. They'd been to several over the course of a day or two. They were traveling to see Rick's family here in Ohio. We're from Florida."

Kent's attentiveness was sharpening with each passing moment. Adrenaline and curiosity washing away the remnants of last night's binge. He pushed aside the beer and went for a water. Francie watched him.

"Rick left me, Detective Ober."

He nodded.

"And I think Sienna took my boy. Detective Ober, no one will listen. The cops won't do anything back home because they say with all the family drama and Rick missing and not answering, that likely Toby is with him. And he's sixteen and had run away a couple of times before, so..." She paused to get her breath. "But I know she took him. I just don't know why or where." Francie broke into sobs, turning her head away from Kent toward the cobweb-ridden wall.

Kent fished out a clean dish rag from the drawer and handed it to his guest before sitting down with a flop. "Malachi started acting odd about the same time the blue showed up in his eyes. Took him to the eye guy. Said a change that drastic had to be a sign of some disease process. Stroke. Hemorrhage. Malachi stopped cooperating, and his mom and I couldn't control him or make him go. Started telling us we didn't understand his kind. The bluer his eyes became the more..."

"In tune?" Francie had gathered herself a little and used the tattered dish rag to wipe her face.

"In tune is a good word." Kent remembered the first day Malachi declared the phone would ring about two seconds before it rang.

Then a few days later, Malachi not only knew that the cell would ring, but who would be on the other line.

Vicky grew scared of him. Felt like he could read her mind. Kent had blown her off initially. Maybe if he'd listened. Paid more attention...

Then he noticed that Malachi knew when Vicky and Kent were awake, asleep. When they were hungry. When they were about to come down with an illness. And as for sleep, well, Malachi stopped requiring any. At least as far as they could tell.

"Sienna became smarter by the day, or so it seemed. Freaked me out. Freaked all of us out. A few months after the cave, she'd become the smartest one in any room she was in. Not book smart, so much. Just a *knowing*. A creepy, deep knowing."

Kent stood again and brought over the rack of test tubes. "Friend of my wife's helped me get this started. I think out of pity, so I don't even know what I'm doing really. I have some samples from the caverns. All three caverns. I don't know which one had the substance or material that Malachi encountered. I test them and change out the reactors from the reactants, I think is what it's called."

Francie picked a couple of tubes up and held them up to the light. "What have you found?"

"One tube, a few weeks ago, glittered with turquoise specks for a brief second when I added a strand of his hair. I've tested and tested, but now I don't have any more DNA from him. I don't know where he is."

She looked at Kent, brown eyes wide, then back down to the tubes. He thought he caught a faint line of a contact lens as he watched for her reaction. She wore her wedding ring and had twisted it on her finger as she'd talked with him. Kent hadn't worn his contacts in several days. He'd lost enough weight that his ring kept falling off, so he'd left it off. What was the point?

"Do you have any samples or..."

"No. I don't have anything like this. I was just lucky enough to find you. To track down anyone that would understand. To help me find where my kids may be."

"What about your husband?"

"What about your wife?" Francie must've seen Kent's startled reaction at her sharp tone and then added, "Sorry. That was out of line."

Kent nodded. "No worries. It's stressful."

"Rick won't answer. Police can't get him to pick up either. Like I said, Toby's ran away before, so no one's really looking." She fingered the tubes again.

"Same with Vicky. She left her position at the college. Friends gave up trying to talk with me about her, too. She's just, gone." At that last sentence, Francie swung her arm out in frustration, sending the tubes spilling and shattering at Kent's feet.

"Oh, my God. I'm so sorry. No, don't touch it!" Her forcefulness stopped Kent from reaching barehanded for the tubes. He'd been careful so far not to get any samples on his skin. He'd given up the respirator after Vicky. If he inhaled it, oh, well.

That bit had let him understand that Malachi had likely touched something or ingested it. But breathing it didn't hurt him. Kent didn't really know if any of the substances he'd sampled were what caused the turquoise eyes and super-brain mentality.

"I'll get a broom."

"Please, Detective. I'll help you clean this up. All of it." She waved her hand toward the cobwebs. "If you'll help me find my kids."

"Ma'am I feel for you. I really do, but I don't even know where my kid is."

She tapped at the broken glass with her tennis shoe. "Accompany me to the caverns. How far is it from here? An hour? I'll help you get more samples. We can ask questions there of the staff. Please, Detective."

The protector-fixer deep inside Kent, the part of him that had made him an excellent investigator, rose to the surface, replacing the aggravation over the lost samples. Her brown eyes pleaded from behind that loose curl and the contact lenses.

He ran down a mental list of what he'd need to do in order to leave the trailer with this woman in his vehicle. Shower. Shave.

Gun and badge.

He shook his head. That last item wasn't even valid any longer. But he didn't know what they'd run into along the way...

He felt for her. All the crying and eye rubbing and nose blowing.

"Give me a minute."

He retreated down the hall to the bathroom and started the shower for the first time in days.

THE TRIP TO CAVE COUNTRY TOOK ABOUT AN HOUR. THEY'D stopped for gas and junk food at the first filling station before pulling onto the winding county road void of middle lane yellow and shoulder whites. He drove, unsure of her backroad driving abilities. Francie had rummaged through his kitchen, washed and retrieved the ancient coffee pot and brewed who-knows-how-old black coffee. Stale and strong enough to use as engine fuel, but it'd sobered him up the rest of the way and gave him the jolt he needed to enter the conspiracy theory world afresh.

He was impressed, albeit a little baffled, with Francie. Her stamina and determination outmatched many driven, frantic mothers he'd dealt with over the years. Most of the moms of runaways, especially older runaways, gave up the physical search a few months in. The mental search was the next to go, when relentless strings of sunrises wouldn't pause long enough to allow enough time for laundry and jobs and the needs of the rest of the family. The emotional pull — the endless soul searching of what went wrong and whose fault and if things had been different — that part. That never ends. Not that he was aware of.

As Kent navigated his pickup around the S-curves and passed slow-moving farm vehicles, the parents shared timelines and tales and tragedy. He was strangely drawn to this woman, but he knew it was more likely their shared predicament. Her petite frame bounced on the bench seat as he hit potholes and rough road. She clung a paisley shoulder bag close to her chest. Occasionally she'd dig out a photo or a document of some sort from the bag, then replace it with great care. Her bag was like Kent's kitchen. Her source of busy work and hope — and hopelessness.

Francie bemoaned the police force in her small hometown for not doing enough. He'd been on the receiving end of those blows over the years. Runaway, at-risk teens from impoverished districts held lower priority for the force than first-timers from affluent suburbs or the younger missing kids. It shouldn't be, but it was the way things are. Not enough resources and manpower to find the missing.

And there were always missing kids.

He and Francie had searched for their kids—and for the reason they changed—for years, each parent believing themselves to be alone in the plight. Optometrists and doctors had no explanation and no solutions. Sienna and Malachi stopped eating. Then sleeping. But the kids didn't deteriorate. Quite the contrary, Malachi had developed a defined muscular frame nearly in a week-all without lifting the first set of dumbbells. Francie reported similar body changes in Sienna. But the intuition to anticipate their parents' next moves and deepest thoughts was more concerning.

Kent became scared of Malachi about three months after his field trip. Francie stopped trusting Sienna sooner, more like two months. Both kids on the same timeline.

Both with brilliant blue eyes. Francie managed one photo of Sienna's eye color change. The flash had hurt the girl's eyes.

Francie had been back to Cave Country, to each of the three cavern systems, three times. No one believed her about her daughter's illness until she'd run into just the right employee.

The same khaki-clad tour guide that Kent had slammed into the side of the visitor's center vending machine in a fit of frustration.

"Yeah. That was a bad day." Kent hoped Francie wouldn't think less of him for that loss of temper. Bad enough what she must think of his hung-over isolation in the filthy single-wide.

"I've had bad days, too." She related how she'd yelled at Toby for no reason and lashed out at her extended family. "Never put anyone into the glass front of a snack food machine, though." She almost smiled.

Ken almost smiled.

Almost.

Ken braked as he came upon the entrance to the empty visitors parking lot—a lot that should be filled with tourists and school groups this time of day. Wooden barricades with peeling yellow paint sat between the two limestone monuments that marked the entry. A streamer of yellow caution tape flapped between the massive stones and around the posted warning sign.

Kent threw the pickup's gear into park and jumped down to the pavement to get a closer look at the sign. Francie followed him, clutching her bag.

White-nosed syndrome. Some fungus being inadvertently carried via human foot traffic into the caves killing off the much-needed bat population. The sign gave maps of incidents and an encyclopedic explanation along with a museum-quality infographic.

"Do you think—"

"No. I already checked into that possibility. This happens every ten years or so. The fungus doesn't hurt humans, or so my biology friend assured me."

Kent returned to the pickup, cursing under his breath for the wasted trip. Francie, though, slung her bag around her shoulder and started pulling down the caution tape and scooting the wooden barricades aside with her hip. "We aren't stopping, Detective. I've come too far."

"Francie, we can come back when—"

"No. You leave if you want. I'm going in." She shot him a look that caused him to take a step back. All she needed were turquoise flames coming from her eyes and her intensity would match that of Malachi's.

A mother in pain, fractured heart. Desperate for answers.

Maybe two heads would be better than one. And better not to run into the employees who knew Kent all-too-well from his demanding tirades in the visitor's center.

Kent caught his breath and readjusted his belt. His fingers reached for the bulge of a badge he no longer carried. He had no jurisdiction here even if his badge were active.

And should he be caught carrying on park property, he'd lose his personal weapon, too.

He fingered the other bulge behind his back and followed Francie into the parking lot.

THE MAIN GATE GUARDING THE TICKET BOOTH GREETED THEM with wrought iron bars and welcome signage wrapped in the middle with a heavy link chain. "Listen, Francie. Let me make a couple of calls and see if—"

Francie dug in her bag and pulled out a lock set.

"Really? You're going to break and enter this facility in front of a police officer?

She smiled at him. The first genuine whole faced smile he'd seen from her. "Yup. And aren't you an ex-police officer?"

Heat rose under Kent's collar. This woman kept surprising him. "There are better ways. I'm already in trouble for—" As he leaned against the gate, blocking her from accessing the padlock, the iron bars swung ever so slightly and the chain gave way, padlock clamoring to the ground. Kent picked up the heavy lock, it's curved shackle had been sawed through.

"I didn't do that," Francie said.

Instinct and years of training brought Kent's hand down to the right side of his belt where his service weapon used to hang. His eyes swept the perimeter, then up to look for cameras. Then he remembered he didn't have his service weapon. His personal weapon nestled against his lower back. He stopped himself before reaching the rest of the way for it. He didn't want to alarm Francie.

Actually, he was afraid if she knew he had it that she'd want to be the one to carry it in.

He pulled on her forearm, gently pushing her behind him and swung the gates open all the way, the chain dangling free from one side. "Probably kids." Kent's buddies on the force used to get calls about kids scaling the fence to go deep into the caves, especially around Halloween and every time the thirteenth fell on a Friday. Partiers. Mostly harmless. A handful of older teens came out of the ordeals with vandalism or trespassing charges.

As the pair eased toward the mouth of the cave past the ropes where tour guides typically stood to direct traffic, Kent caught the faint hint of campfire smoke. He scanned the treetops. A towering monster out of his sight cracked and creaked in the breeze. It was odd to be here with the place vacant. No whining children needing to go potty. No parents yelling for kids to stay close. No rodeo or western music drifting from the gift shop. A few birds put their two-cents worth in and Kent stepped into the mouth followed by Francie.

Kent hadn't been to this part of Cave Country in several months. What Mother Nature does in that time is unreal. A portion of the mouth was shut off with safety cones and more caution tape. A giant boulder had fractured off from the main ceiling and lay in crumbled shards of stone. The well-worn entrance was littered with bits of gravel.

"Watch your step." He kicked a couple of larger rocks to the side of the boulder pile.

The safety bulbs lining the cave's topmost edge remained on all the time, according to the research he'd done. Since it was marked for tourism, it was mandated by first responders and various government officials that even during off seasons and, like now, times when the cave is shut off to the public that the lights stay on.

Kent understood but had to wonder if the pathways drew more vandals this way.

Of the three caverns in this system, this one was still active. Water dripped from root systems above and trickled down the walls and ceilings, carrying with it minerals which made the cave's funky formations and glistening walls. This one was the most popular. Dry caves are not so shiny.

Francie stumbled on an uneven patch, knocking Kent into the wet wall. Their small commotion startled something deep within the cave, and, despite the daylight hour, a couple of angry bats flew out of the mouth and up to the trees above.

"Sorry, Detective."

They readjusted their stride and went further in. "Maybe we get those samples now and get out." Kent nodded toward Francie's bag where he'd stocked her up on fresh test tubes and water droppers for collecting liquids from the cave. "There's a small pool over there."

"Sienna told me she'd gone deeper."

"I thought Sienna didn't tell you anything. I thought by the time you made the cave connection she'd stopped giving you information like that."

Francie grinned and nodded. "Well, this is all fresh. Wouldn't it make sense that whatever did our children harm would've come from deeper in the cave, where the water had a chance to pick up whatever foreign substance caused them to evolve?"

"Evolve?"

"How else would you describe what happened to our kids, Detective? They're stronger, smarter, more in tune. Isn't that the definition of evolution?"

"A survival of the fittest thing?" The fixer-protector part of him took its place in the corner of his mind, giving way to the cynical questioner. The part that made him an excellent interrogator. At least at one point.

Where was this guy when he could've used a clue about Vicky leaving? About his mom's decline?

He followed the lit passageway another thirty feet. The campfire smoke was stronger, wafting into his face from the direction he and Francie were headed.

With the interrogator personality front and center, Kent decided to take a different approach. "When did Rick leave?"

"Why is that important?"

"Just trying to get the timeline straight in my head," Kent lied. The passageway narrowed, making it impossible to walk side by side. He led on. "If we can find as many similarities as possible, maybe the pattern will help us find a cure."

"Cure." She laughed and her voice bounced off the lowering ceiling. They had to duck a stalactite to continue. Her demeanor had changed from frantic searching mother to smug and as cynical as Kent as soon as they'd pulled in front of the parking lot. Or maybe the cynicism had always been there and Kent had been too hungover this morning to notice.

That comment about his wife. How did she know? He didn't wear a ring.

"Cure?" She was saying. "You think that some freak evolutionary event has a cure when we seem to be the only two people who know about it."

"Rick knows. Vicky knows. At least they know some things. They've seen the eyes." Kent paused and wished he'd brought a flashlight. The low-watt bulbs behind their metal cages spaced ten feet apart only lit so much. Somewhere deeper, from the direction of the frail ribbons of smoke, the echoes of a rock or two skidding over stone padded down the passageway. The path had narrowed enough now that if Kent wanted to go back up to the outside, he'd have to make Francie the lead.

He thought he wanted to go back to the entrance. Every part of him that remained Detective Ober wanted to go back to the entrance.

He turned and looked at Francie through the dim. The only light behind her was from the bulbs. The path had snaked and curled so that he couldn't see natural light at all. As if someone had staple-gunned black plastic trash bags to the eastward-facing orifice blocking out all of the sun's rays.

Francie took a step toward him. She'd hung her bag across her tiny body. She took another step. He stepped backward, but kept eye contact with her.

Those contacts. Those brown eyes. Around the edges of her contacts he made out the slightest tinge of blue. Even in the dim. Another step backward for Kent. Another one forward for Francie.

"Rick and Vicky do know. So do the couple of doctors our kids saw. But what good did that do?"

The way she said his estranged wife's name. Like she knew her.

"Did you ever stop to think Malachi was better off? Did you ever stop to think that maybe what happened to him was a blessing?"

"Blessing? Where is this coming from, Francie?"

The blue glow intensified from the rims of her contact lenses. Another step forward for her. Another step backward for him.

"Did you ever want to be a part of something grander than your-self? Than that pathetic existence you have with the unenlightened?" Francie was so close to his chest he could smell the shampoo even in the damp of the cave. Even over the growing strength of burning firewood.

He nodded. Stalling. "Why don't you enlighten me?

She took another half step toward him, and when he made eye contact with her this time, her forehead was even with his nose. "You have the right DNA. You were on the right track, Kent, but we have better plans for you than solving a little bitty cavey mystery."

"And what's that?" He tried not to flinch, but the lack of light and excess of caffeine earlier made him jittery. And that familiar fear Malachi gave off wafted around him like the smoke.

She patted his chest and looked up at him. "Rick and Vicky came around. You will too. And so will the docs."

Kent reached behind for his weapon, but met with icy fingers around his wrist.

He spun and felt Francie close at his back, removing his weapon.

Heard the gun clatter to the ground. Heard her kick it far behind them toward the entrance, metal-on-stone echoing. More rocks falling somewhere. Echoing.

He faced his opponent.

"Hi, Dad." Malachi smiled at him. He blinked his turquoise eyes with their splintered black shards of shattered pupils. "Welcome to the Fracture."

Before Kent could react, Malachi splashed his father in the face with a foul-smelling liquid, then with a swift right hook, the dimly lit cave went all black for Kent.

***

KENT KNEW WHO HE'D BEEN BEFORE. HE KNEW HE SHOULD tell someone before it took him over completely. True to her word, Francie had cleaned and mopped and dusted the secluded single-wide home. Vicky helped. Rick tidied up the lawn. The doctors were on their way after procuring the group various high-end contact lenses.

Malachi was back. Not the son he'd known, but he wasn't the dad Malachi had a few months ago, either.

Or has it been a few years?

Sienna and Toby were in the yard resting by the campfire. Rick and Vicky acted like they'd known each other for a lifetime. All in the party sported the same eyes. The same ways of knowing each other more intimately than one lifetime could allow. Their unity was indescribable—intoxicating—and the fracture hadn't fully taken Kent over yet.

Kent knew he should call for help—his biologist friend, a former partner or two, someone—before the turquoise and black could splinter through his whole iris. Before the change was complete.

But he had his family back. And then some. The urge to isolate, to isolate with this tiny but growing group of people burned brighter in him by the moment. To stick with his kind. Not to fracture their alliance.

He knew better than to retreat. To hole up. To isolate.

He should call someone. Warn them.

Warn the unenlightened of things to come.

As he tore down the black trash bags from the eastward-facing window in his little room, he also knew he was stubborn enough not to.

AS IT HAPPENS

A little sci-fi, a little feel good, follow along with Henrietta Happenstance's plight as she realizes just how uniquely positioned she is to spread joy and hope—no matter where—or when—she might be. First Appearing in <u>Blurred Timelines</u>*.*

Henrietta Happenstance happened to be born in 1841 in an Appalachian Mountain blizzard, and though she'd spent her 67 years on Planet Earth spread out over many more than seven decades, the ever-present and ever-frustrating fight with dandelion seeds mucking up her line drying was enough to make her cuss.

And she'd seen plenty enough in Ray's Hollow to make her cuss.

She grumbled under her breath as she shook loose her bedsheet from the clothesline, then gave the fabric a few more hard flaps to rid it of the white tufts. Dozens and dozens of seeds took to the light breeze, floating about their business and destined to take root in the dry, parched earth. Or in her ever-graying pixie cut which was now sticking to her head from the heat.

Or, as it happens, right back in her clothes basket to aggravate and irritate her even further. Now the blasted tufts were free of the sheet, but nestling in her unmentionables down in the basket.

Dandelions. She couldn't get her grass to grow unless she watered, but then she couldn't keep track of the modern rules and regulations on when irrigation was allowed and when conservation mode was in full effect, so she didn't. She had no desire to borrow trouble from the local lawman, or even Clipboard Carl, who ran himself silly from neighborhood to neighborhood with his clipboard and tickets-in-triplicate, citing this grievance and doling out that fine.

But she'd noticed her neighbor's sprinkler head tsk-tsk-tsking last night and again early this morning.

Carl would be around soon, no doubt. Clipboard and all.

So, as it happens, the weeds grew, but her grass not so much. Not the lush, green blades her family had dreamed of having one day, anyway. She still remembers like it was yesterday—and somewhere, given how things are, it could still be yesterday. Yesterday, when her mother would snuggle her close in their "rented" wagon, the two "rented" mares rigged up and pulling the family away from the harsh mountain life that they could no longer tolerate with three children and one more on the way—due in the winter. Likely would be born in a blizzard. So as her father lightly snapped the reigns, and as the family traveled from one mountain range to another, Mother would dream.

"We'll have grass all around. And so close to the ocean you can hear the waves and taste the salt in the air." Mother would throw her head back a bit, close her eyes and inhale deeply as if she were already standing knee-deep in ocean bathwater.

Mother had gone nuts, just a little, at the arrival of a post sent by her sister, Aunt Marie, and marked from California, glittering with fresh Statehood and twinkling with promise. Even if they didn't happen to hit gold (Aunt Marie and Uncle Milborne had arrived a day late and a dollar or several short), the Happenstances would at least have no more blizzards to deal with. Mother had wanted more children. Many more. And birthing in blizzards was not for her.

So the Happenstances made the trek mostly in that rented wagon with two rented horses that Daddy had lied to the liveryman about and promised to have the set returned by the following weekend. He'd had enough money to pay the rental fee, but not to outright purchase the rig.

The rental turned out to be outright thievery, so Henrietta had thought the family cursed.

And that's how she and her older brother ended up here in the middle of the Sonoran Desert. Ray's Hollow, Arizona. Well, the curse and the lack of general direction of "west." Internal compasses the Happenstances did not have. In Ray's Hollow. Taking seedy laundry off the line in 103-degree heat. And not taking ocean-breeze salty laundry off the line in 70-degree California. Because the Happenstances happened to be cursed. She at the ripe old age of ten, and Marcus being an unfortunate nineteen at the time, when the ground shimmered and trembled ever so slightly at a pit-stop north of Phoenix. North of Phoenix because Mother was fearful of the sin of big cities from all she'd read in Aunt Marie's letters. So they ducked (with no compass internal or otherwise) a jaunt too far south to avoid the blight that was Las Vegas.

South (and back east, quite frankly, showing just how damaged the Happenstances' collective sense of direction was) and north of Phoenix. To Ray's Hollow.

And just like that, the ground opened up and their cacti-laden route to their intended rest at Cacti Cottage Inn in 1851 tumbled the two siblings into a suburb of 1964 bungalows.

Marcus and Henrietta were left to fend for themselves in a foreign future until Marcus was drafted into a war the young Happenstances had no knowledge of. Just like that, Henrietta was orphaned.

A knot came up in her stomach at the recollections. At all the losses suffered in those early years. Ever so grateful that after Marcus left, the kind manager of Cacti Corner took her in in exchange for, of all things, laundry service. Manager Mike and his wife Dorothy loved and raised her as their own. Henrietta questioned this when she was old enough to put things together. Their response, as was the response of most people in these parts when dealing with hard questions, was simple. "Ray's Hollowers stick together. We don't ask questions."

Henrietta would always have a job at Cacti Cottage. And a place to live in one of the rooms if she desired. But she didn't desire that. The inn was more than a little creepy, the rooms never behaving as they should. About the time she learned the layout, a new addition would pop up. Or an entire hallway would cease to exist.

No. Working there was fine, and she was glad for the job.

Living there? She saved up enough to buy a simple bungalow as far from the bustle of town as she could get. Away from the thousands of questions that no one answered except with "Hollowers stick together."

And, as it happened, she'd not needed to scrimp and save. Marcus, prior to his departure for Vietnam, handed little Henrietta the pocket watch their father had entrusted her brother with, along with a trouser pocket full of coins and bills. All of these things she'd innocently handed over to Manager Mike and Dorothy. To pay her debt. Unlike her horse thief of a father. Even at that young age, Henrietta understood the link between sin and consequences.

Looking back, Mike and his wife could've auctioned off those items and bought five hotels along the California coast. But they didn't. They stayed put. And they cashed in and invested those antique relics for modern currency and a savings account for Henrietta.

Once the couple realized her work ethic landed on the positive side of responsibility, and once she'd reached the old age of twenty-five and had moved into her bought-and-paid-for bungalow, the inn's managers sat her down and explained what they'd done with the Happenstance fortune.

And it was a fortune. Mike expected Henrietta to leave his employ, and there'd be no hard feelings. She should travel the world. See what grand hopes and dreams she could muster.

But Henrietta felt such a deep sense of gratitude and belonging at the hotel, that she stayed on. And on and on.

And, as it happens, Cacti Cottage Inn—now under new management, of course—was expecting her in a few hours for a simple shift down in the laundry room. Well, yesterday the laundry room was "down." Today, the facility could be on the top floor.

She stopped asking questions about that ages ago. She went to work, did her job, and returned to her out-of-the-way bungalow.

But, as it happens, her little home wasn't out of the way enough. Turned out, that hole that spit and shimmered and shook and swallowed Marcus and her whole was about ten feet from her very own backdoor in her very own bought-and-paid-for backyard... Thus all the "grandchildren" showing up to spend a few days with Henrietta.

Where future medicine could help children of the past live longer. Forever altering history and time, and...

Thus the necessity of an addition built just off her backyard, overlooking the portal. Standing guard. Thus the purchase of so many baby monitors and, later, live-stream cameras sending images of the back yard portal directly to her smartphone.

A wave of dizziness threatened to topple her off balance. She must be more tired than usual, a side effect of remembering, old age, and that blasted thirst. Henrietta's throat was as parched as the ground as she pulled the last of the pillowcases from the line. She folded it and tossed it into the basket and fished out her water bottle. These days she was never more than an arm's length from that bottle, the dryness in the back of her throat growing more by the day no matter how much she drank. She should visit the clinic again and get the results from her lab tests, but the good folks at Ray's Hollow Medical would ask her about her grandchildren.

She leaned against the clothesline post and finished off the rest of the water, but it wasn't enough. The right back side of her throat was well and stuck to the back left side of her throat.

She went to the spot just past the clothesline as she did multiple times a day. It was closed up tight, much to her relief. She didn't think she had the energy to deal with an ill child today. She dared to put a foot over it and press down. Once, about twenty years ago, when she'd tested the hole with her foot, she'd lost one of her very favorite pumps through the shimmer. Made her cuss, it did. Not that she couldn't afford new shoes, but that she had to imagine someone in another decade coming across a random footwear fashion and tossing the bright blue heel into a garbage pail. Or keeping it as a strange souvenir.

Another wave of dizziness forced her eyes to close and she nearly toppled into the clothesline post. Maybe she'd have to face the clinic workers today after all. Her hands, wrinkled and knobby from decades of laundry duty at Cacti Cottage, tossed the bottle back into the basket. She gathered the laundry basket under one arm and headed for the back door.

She'd have to face the questions about her grandchildren. And as it happens, Henrietta couldn't keep track of the grandchildren. There were far too many coming and going all the time. The names and ages and points of origin were far too confusing for her. They weren't even her grandchildren. Relatives of some sort, yes. Adjacent ancestors, perhaps. Cousins or an aunt. Or, well. Even the most robust of all modern genealogy tracking software couldn't sort out Henrietta Happenstance's family tree.

So she had to lie to the good folks at Medical. For a good reason, she supposed. As good of a reason as her father had lied to the liveryman about the horses. To make a better life for his growing family.

Henrietta supposed she was helping those kiddos have a better life. She figured word got around, or someone had a peek into the hole and figured their child would be better off in the future, where medicine and treatment can more adeptly keep up with illness and injury.

She kept her entire spare bedroom stocked with modern layettes in bright, fashionable colors. Disposable diapers in all sizes. Formula, too—though the kiddos coming through the shimmer had usually never tasted anything but their mother's milk, so feedings were quite the challenge.

Henrietta had to be prepared for anything. They all had needed a quick wash up (and coming from the dusty, bathe-once-a-week mentality of the past to the shower-daily mentality of the now, sometimes the grime was deep-set). She'd change the little one's clothing, cooing and ooing and singing songs her mother had sung—perhaps something that would be familiar to little ears. There was always a note attached to the child's clothing or swaddle explaining the trouble. Fevers that wouldn't abate in a six-month-old. Rusty nail through the foot of a two-year-old toddler. Festering pink eye in a five-day-old. The mother feared blindness for her child.

Simple fixes for the modern world. Life-suckers in their timelines.

After treatment at the clinic, Henrietta would take the child back to her bungalow, wash the original clothing as best she could, and redress the kiddo in their own decade's appropriate attire. She continued the feedings and giving medicine if needed. She'd pen her own note in cursive scroll on paper she'd yellowed by soaking in tea bags, lest a crisp typewritten note on bright white paper draw undue attention to the family in the past. She'd explain what the medicine was and how to administer it or perform treatment with things the parents may have in their more vintage timelines.

Henrietta kept volumes and tomes of books on the old west, prairie medicine, and Arizona in general. She'd become quite the history buff—not because she loved the period, but because she loved the babies coming to and fro from the period.

But it was all lies on her end, nevertheless. And after about seven trips with various "grandchildren" to the clinic, Henrietta stopped keeping track. She never saw the same child a second time, and she had to wonder if the clinic nurses wondered what Henrietta was doing to all these "visiting grandchildren" for them to have such a wide range of maladies. Sometimes two a month.

These children were never more than a few years old, never old enough to understand—or likely to remember—traveling for medical care against the currents of years. Henrietta would simply shrug at the phenomenon, nuzzle the child-of-the-moment against her chest, and offer up one of a dozen excuses that she'd kept in the back of her mind:

"Us Happenstances just have a hard time with our immune systems."

"Us Happenstances have always had trouble with our tonsils."

"Us Happenstances can be quite clumsy."

And, the Ray's Hollower on duty at the medical clinic would stop asking questions, treat the child, and then Henrietta would have a day or two to care for and love a little one before the hole in her yard would open up and she'd send the child back to the time from which he or she came. Or at least that's how she hoped it worked.

She couldn't be certain.

And there was no one to ask.

Each time the ground glistened and sucked the child back to its own timeline, a tiny piece of Henrietta's heart would go with it. Especially the little girl called Ellie with a bad case of staphylococcus infection. Simple for the 2000s, not so much for the 1900s. Tiny toddler Ellie with a head full of blonde curls and the brightest green eyes that, once she was cleared of the infection, sparkled like emeralds. When the shimmer opened up a week later for Ellie to go back to her time, Henrietta's heart nearly broke. That was a few months ago, and her arms ached to hug the wriggling little girl again.

And not being able to help herself, Henrietta scribbled a P.S. to her letter. "As it happens, I adore this little girl. More than I could ever express in words."

Henrietta struggled with the laundry basket to that porch door now. That was good. She was hot and thirsty. And so, so tired. She'd doubt she could carry a child from the portal into the spare bedroom for a wash-up, let alone trek into town with it. And lie.

She checked her back pocket for her phone, but it wasn't there. She glanced over her shoulder toward the clothesline. It must've fallen out...

She managed to get one foot and the basket inside the porch door when another wave of dizziness overtook her. She knew she needed help. She stumbled back to the yard, hoping to reach her phone before she had no more presence of mind to dial the numbers.

She put a hand out on the post nearest the house. A few more steps. She could see the black rectangle lying in the dusty yard. Guarded by a dandelion.

She reached the far post, her knees putty under her weight, put a hand out, slid to the ground, and then...

Nothing.

Bright lights washed over Henrietta's face, the glare burning her cheeks. She was supine on a hard surface. Cold air brushed over her body in great wafts. She blinked, her eyes watering.

She reached up and felt the teardrop and traced its path along her wrinkled cheek. A foreign sensation, she thought, as she'd been so parched for so long that she'd not produced tears heavy enough to fall. Not even when she remembered her family, even Marcus.

She reached up with her other arm, weak and shaky. It was covered in some sort of sleeve. She'd been wearing a sleeveless blouse to undo the laundry. Now she had a sleeve. Tight and smooth to her skin with patterns of ripples. She blinked hard again, bringing her eyes into focus. The sleeve was the brightest purple she'd ever seen. The ripples were like veins running all up and down. Her other arm was still bare. She glanced down to see the peach of her summer top. Still in her own clothes. Just a wild purple sleeve.

"Henrietta? Are you okay?" A harsh, hushed whisper near her head. "I didn't know what to do. I tried to pull and tug you into the porch to cool you off, but, well…"

Henrietta, still foggy and barely comprehending, "Where am I?"

"The clinic."

She took a deep breath. She didn't smell the familiar antiseptic wash of the Ray's Hollow Medical offices— a scent that was burned into her nostrils after dozens of visits with the children. She smelled something else—clean like lavender, calming but not overpowering. No chemical smells at all. The sleeve on her arm tightened and she felt that much more clear-headed.

"What clinic?"

"Ray's Hollow."

She raised up to one arm and the owner of the hushed, harsh whisper came to her aid. A clank on the table behind her caused her to turn. There next to her was Clipboard Carl's clipboard. She blinked again. And there was Carl.

She tried to pull away, but Carl steadied her.

"Like I said," he whispered again, "I was in the neighborhood, your neighbors, they…" he picked up his clipboard, then set it down with a clank again next to her. "Well. That's no matter. I found you collapsed in the backyard. I tried to right you on your feet. To get you to come to, but, well. The shimmer and shake and now. Well…"

"Both of us? Through that tiny hole?" Realization made Henrietta's skin prickle, gooseflesh giving birth to gooseflesh. "When are we, Carl? *When?*"

"I don't know. Future. Not back. Not old times. Man, I did that once, luckily the shimmer and shake was still opened and I hopped back in. That happened in Old Man Wicker's—"

"Carl!" Sometimes this man was worse than dealing with dandelion seeds. The nervous type. She'd dated him once, eons ago, enough to turn her off men for a good long while. "Focus."

"I don't know. I just called for help when we came through and the neighbor called the ambulance." He leaned in closer. "They let me ride with you. I told them I was your beau."

Henrietta moaned.

"Henrietta. The ambulance didn't have wheels." He leaned in close and whispered. "It floated."

"Are you sure we're in Ray's Hollow?" Even with all the odd happenings, hovering vehicles seemed like a stretch for a town so small. Maybe down in Phoenix in the future. But Ray's? Carl pointed to the wall. A hologram in purple and yellow spun and twisted with information. Henrietta's name. A "Welcome to Ray's Hollow Medical, Where Your Care Is Our Pleasure" scrolled underneath her vital signs. At least her heart was beating. At least she was breathing.

The sleeve on her arm tightened and loosened over and over. It didn't hurt. It felt calming, and with each squeeze, she became more alert—and less thirsty.

The door opened and a nurse clad in bright purple from head to toe smiled warmly. She was young, perhaps early twenties. Blonde curls poked out from under a medical cap. "Henrietta Happenstance. It's a pleasure to see you up and alert. You were quite the sick lady. Let's see." She turned to the wall and whisked her hand over the screen without touching anything. "Your labs look much better now. When you came in a few hours ago, your throat was riddled with a nasty staph infection. We've not seen a case like yours in ages. One for the history books, that's for sure." She turned and winked at me.

With eyes shimmering like emeralds.

Ellie.

She knows.

She knows about the holes and the shimmers and the shakes. Ellie.

"Oh my." Henrietta managed. She'd sent little Ellie into the future and not at all back to her parents.

"Oh my." Henrietta's stomach wrenched into a knot. The heartache those folks must've had over the loss of their little girl. No wonder another child hadn't come through in so many weeks. The folks in the past must've thought that the lady on the other side who'd helped so many tykes had kidnapped their daughter.

"Oh no." Carl started patting her shoulder, but Henrietta shrugged him off. He must think her to be distraught over the diagnosis. Or the time travel. But she was a wreck over the baby mix up.

The nurse smiled and turned back to the wall. "And mercy, were you dehydrated. What were you doing to become so ill and not take care of yourself?"

Carl piped up. "I think she was doing laundry. Bringing it in from the line."

The nurse tilted her head and furrowed her brow. "From the line? What line?"

Henrietta, her head clearer by the second which allowed her intense worry more wriggle room, intervened. "Chores. I was doing chores outside. In the heat. What is your name, dear?"

The nurse smiled and placed a hand on Henrietta's. "Carl," she said to him. "Would you give Henrietta and me a moment? There's water and coffee in the foyer." He nodded and started out the door. "Wait."

He paused.

"Here. You'll need this." She handed him a card from her scrub pocket. It shimmered like the hologram on the wall. And with her own whisper she added, "As it happens, your money won't work here." Carl, clutching his clipboard to his chest with one hand and holding the card up to the light with the other, left us alone in the room.

The nurse sat next to Henrietta on the table. The young lady smelled of lavender, like the air, only sweeter. "I've read about you. I've seen your note you left with my mother the day you sent her completely healed back through time. I've kept that letter all these years."

It was Henrietta's turn to furrow her brow and tilt her head in confusion. She'd have sworn this was Ellie. But this was Ellie's *child*. "What year is it? You can't possibly be Ellie's little girl."

"You do live in Ray's Hollow, right? We don't ask questions. And the questions we do ask have so many different answers that we can't figure it out. We just move along life, as it happens, floating in and out of time like, well, like dandelion seeds on the wind. Always seeking a new place to grow and thrive. To wish for better lives for all of us."

Henrietta could only nod. This girl's take on dandelion seeds— and that dandelions hadn't been eradicated here in... when was she again? "What year is it? What's your name?"

"Oh, I'm sorry. There I go. Being one of those that doesn't answer questions right away. Habit, I guess. The year is 2106, and my name is Emily."

"Emily. 2106." Math was never Henrietta's strong suit. Timeline math in Ray's Hollow could drive one to drinking. "So somewhere, sometime, you got separated from your mom? From Ellie?"

"Yes, I did. That's a long story. One to be recorded in the Ray's Hollow Record Hall, for sure. Mother lived a long and happy life, according to the archives I've read. And that's thanks to you. Thanks to your willingness to pour time and love and modern medicine into sick little kids." She reached for my arm and removed the healing sleeve in one gentle motion. Emily brushed a tear away that Henrietta hadn't realized escaped. They were flowing freely now, the hydration must be back online.

Emily stood and faced Henrietta. "And now, it's been my true pleasure to do the exact same for you." She held out her arms, embraced the older lady and kissed the top of her head—much like Henrietta had embraced Ellie and kissed that mop of blond curls not so long ago.

"And now, let's get you back where you belong—you and your ever-so-skittish Mr. Carl—before the good-intentioned clueless ones starts asking their own set of unanswerable questions."

It was too fast. Henrietta wanted to stay here with her. Even on this hard table in this harsh light. She wanted to breathe in more lavender and take in more emerald glances. It was too fast.

Emily sensed her hesitation. "You've got work to do in your time-line. I've got work to do in mine." Wise beyond her years, Henrietta knew the young nurse was right. There was work to do. "Where, how?" Henrietta never knew when the portal would open on her own property.

"We've come a long way in understanding some things. And some things don't change. Head down the street to the Cacti Cottage. Room 782. But hurry. The room won't stay there past the end of the afternoon."

"Room 782. There's no seventh floor—" Henrietta stopped herself. She knew good and well that the cottage could have as many floors as it wished to have. "Thank you. Emily. Thank you." The ladies embraced again, and Henrietta went to collect Clipboard Carl and make the portal.

On their way, just a few blocks-worth of travel, they admired the hovering automobiles, the sparkle of the Phoenix skyline in the distance—the skyline was much the same, only shinier. And instead of airplanes circling for a landing, great blimps and hot air balloons dotted the sky. What a world!

At her feet, the sidewalk was pristine and swirled with purples and teals like abalone shell, but she doubted that's what it was. Likely a material with a name that hadn't been invented yet. Marking the corners of each block, strong healthy saguaro cacti welcomed them. Their massive arms sported clusters of white blooms, as if wearing their best Sunday morning bonnets.

All along the sidewalk were octagonal flower containers in matching purples and teals. And in them, of all things, bloomed bright yellow dandelions, interspersed with stems topped with tufts of seeds as big around as a softball, ready to shed their wishes and dreams into the clean air.

Henrietta took it all in and smiled. And she was glad. Glad she'd stayed in Ray's Hollow. Glad she'd helped all those kiddos live a bit longer somewhere, sometime. A second chance to grow and wish and dream.

She was glad for the kindness and smarts of Manager Mike and Dorothy. Glad she was able to send money back to the liveryman's family many generations later to pay for two stolen horses and a buggy rig. With interest.

Even glad that Clipboard Carl was such a stickler for modern grass-watering penalties. Who knows what would've happened had he not found her, even if the falling into the time slip was an act of sheer clumsiness.

Carl followed her gaze as Henrietta stopped to smell the dandelions. "You think we should tell them they're propagating an invasive species?" Carl fiddled with his clipboard like it was his security blanket.

"No." Henrietta picked a stem with a perfectly round ball of white tuft as big as her fist. She blew the seeds, and she and Carl paused on their way to the shimmer and shake portal at Cacti Cottage, room 782, just for a moment to watch the dandelion seeds float on the Arizona breeze. "I think, as it happens, we should let them keep on wishing."

ABOUT THE AUTHOR

Beth enjoys chucking words into sentences then standing back to see what magic—or mayhem—falls out, crafting tales in mystery, sci-fi, fantasy, and general "slice of life" fiction. She couldn't accomplish this without the help of her tutu-clad Little Miss Muse and Trudi the Concrete Office Goose, who's partial to superhero capes.

Her stories have appeared in multiple publications, including Pulphouse Fiction Magazine and Ellery Queen Mystery Magazine, and in multiple fiction anthologies. She's received several Honorable Mentions from Writers of the Future. Her lighthearted blog peeks into the writing life as she pokes fun at herself and her circus of a life.

Follow the antics of Little Miss Muse and Trudi, read Beth's blog (she might have burned down her kitchen last week), and discover the stories at bapaul.com.

Short Story Collections

Spunk and Spice, Volumes 1 and 2: A Collection of six short stories celebrating timeless wit and wisdom.

Out There, Volumes 1 and 2: A Collection of six short sci-fi and speculative tales.

Mystery Minutes, Volumes 1 and 2: Six short mystery stories

All the Feels, Volumes 1, 2, and 3: Collections of inspiring short stories

Just a Tick of Whimsy, Volumes 1 and 2: Collections of fantasy shorts.

Hijacked Holidays: Definitely not your warm-and-fuzzy winter tales.

Dark Minds: Toe-curling twisted mysteries.

Blog Compilations: Slices of the writing life with lots of laughs and bumps in the road.

Life Along the Way

Life All Over Again

Novels

Triage

Young Adult (or Young at Heart) Books

Switch: Book 1 in the Oliver Andrews Trilogy